Anonymous

Life of Henry Clay, the statesman and the patriot : containing numerous anecdotes

With illustrations

Anonymous

Life of Henry Clay, the statesman and the patriot : containing numerous anecdotes
With illustrations

ISBN/EAN: 9783337306366

Printed in Europe, USA, Canada, Australia, Japan

Cover: Foto ©Raphael Reischuk / pixelio.de

More available books at **www.hansebooks.com**

THE YOUNG AMERICAN'S LIBRARY.

LIFE

OF

HENRY CLAY,

THE STATESMAN AND THE PATRIOT.

CONTAINING

NUMEROUS ANECDOTES.

With Illustrations.

BOSTON:
LEE AND SHEPARD, PUBLISHERS.
NEW YORK:
LEE, SHEPARD AND DILLINGHAM.
1875.

PREFACE.

THE biography of Henry Clay is the history of his country, during the term of years that it embraces. But, although he was a constant actor in public life, his sphere did not embrace such stirring events on the ocean and the battle-field, as give the lives of many other American public men their interest.

Mr. Clay's history is the history of the Legislation of the United States; and we have labored so to present it, that our young readers may be introduced to a portion of the annals of their country, which is not usually embraced in brief and compendious narratives.

His personal history, particularly that of his early years, is an incentive to labor and diligence; for what he accomplished, was won with less educational advantages, than most of our young readers possess.   And yet, by diligence, "The Mill-Boy of the Slashes," became, as a brother Senator happily styled him, "*Primus inter Illustres*,"—the Prince of the Senate.   He held this position not by the accident of birth, for his parentage was obscure—not by the favor of partisans, for he was often in the minority—not by talent alone, for natural powers, uncultivated, betray their possessor.   To natural parts, aided by industry, Henry Clay owed his usefulness and his fame.   A nation honors him; for the influence of his mind has guided the progress of his country—felt as that influence has been even while unacknowledged.   And it will moreover be perpetual; for it established customs and rules which have survived the founder, and will endure as long as the republic.

CONTENTS.

~~~~~~~~~

CHAPTER VI.

CHAPTER VII.

CHAPTER VIII.

CHAPTER IX.

CHAPTER X.

CHAPTER XI.

CHAPTER XII.

BIRTH-PLACE OF CLAY.

THE LIFE

OF

HENRY CLAY.

CHAPTER I.

BIRTH AND BOYHOOD OF HENRY CLAY—HIS SCHOOLING—
HIS CLERKSHIP IN RICHMOND—ENTERS THE OFFICE OF
THE CLERK OF THE HIGH COURT OF CHANCERY.

HENRY CLAY was born in Hanover County, Virginia, April 12th, 1777; and thus entered the world at a time when his first perceptions and thoughts would arise from the new order of things, or be drawn toward the republican usages of the new era. By this training he became, in after years, a fit successor to the statesmen who had guided his native country through a long and weary struggle, terminating in a dearly purchased peace, the proclamation of which was among his earliest recollections.

There were many things in the circumstances of his birth, which were conducive to his future usefulness and success. Upon the foundation of a house depends the strength of the structure; and upon the childhood of the man is built his future character. To show how from obscurity and without the aid of wealth, connections, or what are usually deemed the advantages of life, Henry rose to a fame and position second to few in the republic, will be the chief purpose of this biography. Our young readers should be stirred to generous emulation; and as Henry Clay never received the high political reward which is painted as the summit of American ambition, those who read his life should learn the value of that solid reputation, and calm self-respect, which is the substantial recompense of true patriotism. They should from his history learn to appreciate the consciousness of rectitude which can console the possessor even under the attacks of calumny, and which can take away the bitterness of disappointment, even when to defeat there seems to be added the sting of ingratitude. Accident may place the undeserving on the highest pinnacle of human honor; but no accident can confer that highest of worldly rewards—the innate sense of worth — which depends upon no popular verdict, and can be taken away by no human injustice, and destroyed by no ungrateful neglect.

When, in 1783, peace was proclaimed, Henry Clay was in his seventh year, and had been for about two years forced into that state of early and trying independence which a lad inherits who early loses his father; for Henry's father died in 1781. He was a clergyman, and in the humble worldly lot of a self-denying servant of God, has left no memorial which places his name on the record of distinguished men. But he was remembered while those lived whose recollections went back to the period of his life, as a man estimable and beloved in his social relations; and the fame of his son will carry down to posterity the pleasant memory of the man whose early instructions — so soon interrupted — formed the germ of the future excellencies of Henry's character.

But though the death of a father is a great misfortune, there is relief for it in the manly development of character, and the bringing forward of mental strength, which are the effect of the care of a widowed mother. Though her sway be gentle, yet in the case of children thus bereaved we often read Sampson's riddle — out of weakness cometh strength. The boy during his father's life is dependent; but to the feebleness of his mother he becomes a protector; and is early taught of what value even a child, disposed to be obedient and useful, may prove in the world. The mother of Henry Clay lived to see her son realize the reward of his early industry and studiousness, and his filial piety. She survived until 1827, at which date Mr. Clay had been for over twenty years in public life. She watched with a mother's honest exultation his upward progress; and with a mother's deep affection rejoiced that public duties never estranged his heart from his domestic relations, or quenched the sacred feeling of filial piety and obedience.

A favorite symbol during the election of 1844, when Henry Clay was a candidate for the Presidency, was a ruddy lad, mounted upon a horse, with a sack for a saddle. This referred to his early boyhood, when, in common with thousands of his young countrymen, he performed his part in the labors of the house and the homestead. A cardinal requisite to success in life is industry; and a right understanding of what is honorable and what is dishonorable, will lead young and old never to be ashamed of necessary labor. Far

THE VILLAGE SCHOOL.

less will the truly honorable boy or man save his own fancied dignity by imposing undue labor upon mother or sister. There is no more noble trait of character than generosity; and he who sacrifices pride, or overcomes indolence for the assistance of others, is more truly generous, in his self-denial, poor though he be, than if he could throw away, with lavish hand, money which he need not count. And the lad Henry Clay, when a bare-footed messenger between the house and mill, no doubt felt more content than when in later years he bore the public burthen.

The early school advantages of Henry Clay appear to have been very small. His teacher's name was Peter Deacon, and Mr. Clay often referred to him with respect and affection. It does not appear that Henry had any school opportunities after the age of fourteen years. The school-house in which he acquired the elements of reading, writing, and arithmetic, was a rude log structure, having no glass windows—if indeed it had any window whatever. It is said that the only aperture through which light entered was the open door. Henry went forward in his arithmetic as far as " Practice," a rule which, in the old style of teaching, was just far enough from

"units under units, and tens under tens," to enable the pilgrim among figures to "see through"
the book. No doubt Henry was very studious
under Mr. Deacon's tuition; and probably his
father's library, or what remained of it after his
decease, was useful to him. His mother and
elder brothers and sisters, for Henry was the
seventh child, must have aided him in his progress. Home education does often more than can
be accomplished in the few hours daily spent in
school. Many hours every day under a strange
instructor, will do little, if the familiar voices at
home do not cheer and encourage the beginner;
and apparently small opportunities, if home influence is favorable, will produce great results.

At the age of fourteen, Henry Clay was placed
in the store of Mr. Richard Denny, in Richmond,
Va. Nearly all boys can recollect the ordeal
through which they were required to pass, on
leaving the familiar objects at home, and passing
the scrutiny of other and older lads. At school,
or in a store, a shop, or an office, the consciousness
of awkwardness, and want of habitude to the new
occupation, shows the novice to ill advantage.
The older and accustomed clerks, apprentices, or
students, do not hesitate to make a butt of the

new comer. It was a discipline through which they themselves passed, and they are not disposed to lose their revenge, by forbearing to inflict the same annoyance on their successors.

In the store of Mr. Denny, Henry remained for a year. We have no record of the manner in which he spent his leisure time, if he found any, and can only judge by his conduct afterward, and by the results of his life. He says of his own education that it was "neglected, but improved by his own irregular exertions, without the benefit of systematic instruction." In this remark— uttered as an apology for the deficiencies which he felt more than others perceived — we are not to suppose that he intended any reflection upon the mother whose memory he so much revered. She did all that a parent could, under such disadvantages as beset her path. Nor was Mr. Clay forgetful of the kindness of Captain Henry Watkins, to whom his mother was married while Henry was yet young. This gentleman took a father's care of his wife's older children, and to his kindness and influence Henry was indebted for the propitious circumstances which opened to him the career in which he afterwards distinguished himself.

Captain Watkins procured for Henry Clay, at the age of fifteen, a clerkship in the office of Peter Tinsley, Esq., Clerk of the Court of Chancery in Richmond. This was considered a highly eligible position for a lad, and it was no small testimony to Henry's diligence that he was competent to fill it. Probably the other clerks had enjoyed opportunities of learning far superior to Henry's; and this spurred the new comer to studiousness to overcome the distance between himself and them. And if his first appearance in Richmond was a trial to his nerves, the taking possession of his desk in the office of the Clerk of Chancery must have been much greater. He had in dress, manners, and general appearance, all the awkwardness to which we have already referred; for a year in a store could not transform a studious boy into a town lad. His very awkwardness of manner was in reality a testimony in his favor. Any quick, but superficial boy, can soon appear "to the manner born" among lads who have lived in a circle which gives superficial polish; but he whose mind is occupied with graver pursuits, may long be the object of the ridicule of his inferiors.

We are not, then, surprised to learn that the

first impression of the other clerks was, that in the Mill-Boy of the Slashes they were to have a fine object for their practical jokes, and a victim for their pleasantries. The boy had not a hand-some, perhaps not even an agreeable face. His movements were awkward; his dress was rustic —the product of the labor of his good mother— home-spun cloth, made up without the artistic skill of a town tailor. His little coat, which she without doubt had smoothed, and adjusted, and admired, had any thing but a "city set;" and in his clean and well-starched linen, no doubt the little fellow felt all the consciousness of something which he must "keep nice." But the office lads soon discovered that the young rustic was no butt for them, and that whoever encountered Henry Clay in a war of wit and repartee, would find no small antagonist.

Whatever awkwardness the lad felt among those awe-inspiring rows of books and desks in the Chancery Clerk's office, we are sure he could not have felt for one moment ashamed of his parents, or disposed to undervalue their kindness which had placed him there. Perhaps his ardent devotion to the system of "Home Industry," may have had its origin in the Slashes of Hanover, where he early learned what economy and indus·try can accomplish, with small means and against adverse fortune; and if he was not proud of his home-spun clothes, he was glad that his mother had not robbed her own comforts, or incurred debts, to equip him, above her pecuniary means. We cannot conclude this chapter better than by copying a sentiment offered at a Fourth of July dinner, in Campbell County, Va., by Mr. Robert Hughes:—"Henry Clay,—he and I were born close to the Slashes of Old Hanover. He worked bare-footed, and so did I; he went to mill, and so did I; he was good to his mamma, and so was I. I know him like a book, and I love him like a brother!"

CHAPTER II.

YOUNG CLAY AS A STUDENT — CHANCELLOR WYTHE — HIS
FRIENDSHIP FOR THE YOUNG STUDENT — HIS REMOVAL
TO LEXINGTON — HIS OWN REVIEW OF HIS EARLY. LIFE.

HENRY CLAY was what may be termed an extra
clerk in the office of Mr. Tinsley; for when he
was taken in, there was no vacancy. The favor
was procured at the earnest solicitation of his
friends. If he had been idle, or negligent, or
inefficient, it will readily be supposed that he
could not have retained his place. He was put
to the task of copying—and of all drudgery, that
of writing off the interminable words of legal
documents, is to a lad most tiresome. Correctness
and clean writing are required; blots, misspelling,
and interlineations, cannot be tolerated. And
although lawyers themselves are proverbial for
bad penmanship, the clerks who copy documents
for reference or for record, must write a clean and
legible hand. He soon won the respect of his
office companions, and although the youngest

clerk, his superior abilities gave him precedence in their regard. He did not buy their good opinion by partnership in their follies. He was not merely a "pleasant fellow;" for when the others, out of office hours, devoted themselves to amusement, Henry Clay applied himself to his books. He was a most assiduous student, and verified in his experience the fact that change of occupation is relief and rest. Many young men seek in vain for recreation in the excitement of the theatre, or even more questionable places; laboring harder, and fatiguing the mind and body more in the pursuit of amusement, than they would in the calm prosecution of some useful employment. Henry Clay had a higher ambition than to remain a copyist of the results of the legal knowledge of others. He filled up his leisure in study. The hints of erudition which he obtained in his routine of occupations, caused him to thirst for knowledge, and to its acquisition he applied himself with earnestness.

Merit ensures success. Among those whom business brought frequently into the office of Mr. Tinsley, was a venerable man whose own life and experience recommended to his notice the struggles of the boy into whose history he had inquired.

Himself left an orphan at an early age, he knew the dangers and difficulties of such a position. In his case, they rose from the uncontrolled possession of great wealth—more dangerous, perhaps, than the temptations of poverty. He could see the lures to dissipation which surrounded the young, and he admired the steadiness with which Henry resisted them. He knew what industry could accomplish; for after having wasted the years which are usually devoted to education, he had commenced in manhood to recover the time he had lost; and so successfully had he labored, that at the time of which we speak he was sole chancellor of the state of Virginia, a trust which he filled for twenty years — without reproach — without suspicion. Conspicuous before the Revolution, in the Virginia Legislature, as an ardent patriot; a delegate to the first Congress; a signer of the Declaration; a member of the Convention which formed the federal Constitution;—George Wythe was a friend of whom a young man might well be proud. His patronage and direction developed the character of the young clerk, and the employments which he assigned to him increased, while in a degree they met, the thirst for knowledge which kept alive the ambition of Henry Clay.

Chancellor Wythe procured from Mr. Tinsley the services of Henry Clay, as an occasional secretary, to copy his decisions. At length he became, in effect, the private secretary of the Chancellor, though nominally in Mr. Tinsley's office. The studies of Chancellor Wythe were prosecuted with great industry and far-reaching research; in learning, industry, and sound judgment, he had few superiors; and for a lad like Henry Clay to be such a man's private secretary was itself an education. And not only in strictly legal knowledge, but in the classics, in history, in polite literature, the friendly advice of the Chancellor was the guide of the young clerk. Under such judicious instruction, Henry Clay was so trained that he was more than able to cope with his compeers, who received the benefits of education in Universities. He was a continual student, needing only suggestive advice; and he rewarded counsel by obedience, thus encouraging his friends to direct him. Nothing is more discouraging to one who wishes well to a youth, than to find him inattentive to the directions of his elders. No labor was thus lost upon Henry

Clay. He not only availed himself of the kind-ness of his friends, but remembered their good offices with gratitude, and referred to them with emotion, when he had reached a position in which he no longer needed patronage or advice, but could confer both.

Many youth read — but their reading may be desultory; without any established aim, and per-haps with no higher object than amusement. Henry Clay read with an object, as is evident from the fact that when his name had been en-rolled for about a year only, as a student of law, in the office of Attorney-General Brooke, he was admitted to practice by the Court of Appeals. It is not to be supposed that one year could con-fer knowledge of law sufficient to entitle a minor to admission to the Bar, and we therefore infer that the reading of the lad always was of a prac-tical and useful character. For five years young Clay enjoyed the privilege of Chancellor Wythe's friendship; and he was furthermore introduced into the society and notice of John Marshall, afterward Chief Justice of the United States, and other distinguished men of that era. He had thus an opportunity of acquiring, at the fountain-head, a knowledge of the meaning of the founders of the republic, in the constitution which they drew up, and the laws which were passed in pursuance of it. His intimate relation with these political patriarchs, apprised him of the cost of that Union with which his life may be said to have begun; and in his after life he showed himself, on more than one important occasion, the effective friend of his country, and its able defender, whether the threatening danger came from foreign foes, or arose from internal difficulties.

We cannot pass this period in the life of our hero, without commending the example of the young man who sought to improve his mind by listening to the wisdom of his seniors, rather than to dissipate his time and talents in amusement with his fellow-students. He thus secured the esteem of men who could appreciate his character, and predict his success. His relations with those of his own age were also of an elevating character. Like seeks like — and with other young men like himself, studious and ambitious, he combined amusement with instruction in the exercises of a debating society; which was the first scene of his capacity for oratory and for argument. The promise of his life early developed itself; and we may add also that his capacity for winning and securing friends was also early manifested. His frank and generous nature had none of the *finesse* and art which can secure advancement by duplicity and management. He had not the small ambition which can stoop to flattery and fawning, but his character was stamped with an early manliness which commands respect while it invites affection.

After obtaining admission to the Bar, Henry Clay removed to Lexington, Kentucky, in 1797. His parents had preceded him in emigration to that State. The following brief review of his boyhood is extracted from a speech made by him in 1842, when he met some of his old friends at an entertainment, upon his retirement, as he supposed, from public life. " In looking back upon my origin and progress through life, I have great reason to be thankful. My father died in 1781, leaving me an infant of too tender years to retain any recollection of his smiles or endearments. My surviving parent removed to this State in 1792, leaving me, a boy of fifteen years of age, in the office of the High Court of Chancery, in the city of Richmond, without guardian, without pecuniary support, to steer my course as I might or could. A neglected education was improved by my own irregular exertions, without the benefit of systematic instruction. I studied law principally in the office of a lamented friend—the late Governor Brooke —then Attorney-General of Virginia, and also under the auspices of the venerable and lamented Chancellor Wythe, for whom I had acted as amanuensis. I obtained a license to practise the profession from the Judges of the Court of Appeals of Virginia, and established myself in Lexington, in 1797, without patrons, without the favor or countenance of the great or opulent, without the means of paying my weekly board, and in the midst of a Bar distinguished by eminent members. I remember how comfortable I thought I should be, if I could make one hundred pounds, Virginia money, per year, and with what delight I received the first fifteen shillings fee. My hopes were more than realized—I immediately rushed into a successful and lucrative practice."

CHAPTER III.

LEXINGTON DEBATING SOCIETY — THE KENTUCKY BAR — PARTY EXCITEMENT — WASHINGTON AND ADAMS — FOREIGN EMISSARIES — FRENCH AGGRESSIONS — APPREHENDED WAR WITH FRANCE — THE ALIEN AND SEDITION ACTS.

MR. CLAY did not immediately enter upon the practice of law in Lexington, but allowed some months to pass in farther preparatory studies, before he applied for admission as a practitioner. He had a guarantee of success in his modest estimate of his own acquirements; and knowing the distinguished men with whom he would have to cope, he preferred to wait and discipline his mind by application, and to review and systematise the studies which he had pursued with industry, but not with method.

An amusing anecdote is related of this part of his life. There was a debating society in Lexington, of which Mr. Clay of course became a member. His purposes in life, and his associations, would naturally lead him to embrace all helps to the acquirement of experience in speaking, and no opening was to be neglected which would enlarge his circle of acquaintance, and introduce him to those most likely to be of benefit to him.   One evening, as the debate was about to close, Mr. Clay remarked to those who sat near him, that "he did not think the subject had been exhausted."   The observation was overheard, and by universal consent, Mr. Clay was called upon to speak.   He had never spoken in Lexington, and probably never in Richmond, except in the debating club there; and the call of his friends caused him no small feeling of embarrassment. "Mr. Clay will speak!" said one or two members to the chairman; and as he had hinted that there remained something yet to say, he was placed in a dilemma from which he could only escape by saying it.   The chairman nodded to the new member — all eyes were turned upon him in expectation, and all voices were hushed as he rose. "Gentlemen of the jury"—Mr. Clay commenced, and ashamed of his ludicrous error, could not proceed.   But the politeness of the chairman, and the courtesy of the members, who withheld even the pardonable mirth which such a mistake

THE DEBATING SOCIETY.

might well occasion, reassured him. But he began again "Gentlemen of the jury"—and yet again made the same inappropriate commence-ment. As he must now speak, having risen, he persevered, and convinced his hearers that the subject was not, indeed, yet exhausted. Many who heard him that night, and others who heard of the awkward commencement of a brilliant speech, were in the habit, while they lived, of contrasting this maiden effort with the uncon-strained and brilliant speeches which afterward fell from Henry Clay, the finished orator and able statesman.

This first speech in Lexington, notwithstanding its awkward commencement, must have been a very striking performance, and no doubt did much in opening Mr. Clay's path to the practice of his profession. One of the gentlemen who heard it, was in the habit of declaring that the debating club speech was the best that Mr. Clay ever made in his life! He was young, ambitious, and sensitive, and deeply felt the importance of first impressions to his success on a new scene. The commencement "gentlemen of the jury" betrayed his secret, and exposed the fact how busily he had prepared unspoken speeches, and

3

how fixed his mind was upon the profession which he had selected. It was acknowledging that he had *studied* — and to fail would be to betray the fact that he had studied to little purpose. But he nerved himself, and succeeded.

If the young lawyer felt diffident upon entering the profession of law on account of his estimation of the talents of the members of the Kentucky Bar, time has shown that his appreciation of his competitors was not exaggerated. Nicholas, Brackenridge, Hughes, Brown, Murray, Rowan, and others; men who have been conspicuous in the judiciary—in the National and State Legislatures—in foreign embassies—and in the walks of public life at home, were among his associates. And his own life has presented a career as distinguished as that of any of his contemporaries. Some of these men had already achieved reputation when Henry Clay entered the lists with them; and others rose with him to eminence and note. There is no school for youth more improving than a generous and honorable rivalry; and he is sure best to succeed whom choice or circumstance places among those with whom it is an honor to contend.

During these early days in the history of the

republic, master minds had great subjects with which to grapple. Perhaps these very subjects made the men, developing and strengthening their natural powers, and requiring more various knowledge than in more settled times. Every thing was new; and what is now determined by custom, had then to be established upon its own merits. The Presidency of Washington, and of John Adams, was a stormy period. Even the high veneration which the nation felt for the Father of his country, did not prevent his motives from being assailed, and his character aspersed, with a violence and rancor unexceeded in modern party warfare. In a letter to Mr. Jefferson, in 1796, President Washington wrote very feelingly upon this subject of party bitterness:—

"Until within the last year or two, I had no conception that parties would, or even could, go the lengths I have been witness to; nor did I believe until lately that it was within the bounds of probability—hardly within those of possibility —that while I was using my utmost exertions to establish a national character of our own, inde- pendent, as far as our obligations and justice would permit, of every nation of the earth; and wished, by pursuing a steady course, to preserve this country from the horrors of a desolating war, I should be accused of being the enemy of one nation, and subject to the influence of another; and, to prove it, that every act of my administration would be tortured, and the grossest and most insidious misrepresentations of them be made, by giving one side only of a subject, and that too, in such exaggerated and indecent terms as could scarcely be applied to a Nero — to a notorious defaulter — or even to a common pickpocket."

This is strong language. That it was not the effect of mere feeling, there are unfortunate proofs extant, in the contemporary newspapers, and the correspondence of the period — in the debates of Congress, and in the votes barely supporting the President, which are on record. The nation of which he was accused of being the enemy, was France; and that under the influence of which he was said to act, was Great Britain. Time has removed party prejudice, and no man of any party now presumes to doubt the purity and integrity of George Washington; and even the measures which were unpopular during his life, it is conceded were fittest for that period. What he endeavored to do, as he claims in the above paragraph, it is now admitted that he performed, and very much more. His acts and his measures form the precedents or examples upon which the government is now conducted. But this could not be the case without loss to the present popularity of the man who dared to do what he thought right, at any personal sacrifice.

The "exaggerated and indecent terms" in which President Washington was assailed, grew principally out of opposition to the determined stand of neutrality which he took in relation to the wars which followed the French Revolution; and it is matter of history that those who attacked him were directly or indirectly in the French interest. There was everything to prejudice a generous people against Great Britain, and in favor of France. With the one nation, the country had but recently been at war; and the other was the friend and ally of America in her struggle. But the discernment of Washington could not be blinded as to the character of the revolutionary government of France, or the tendency of the wholesale innovations in religion, order, and law, which the reckless fury of the French Revolution proposed and attempted. He feared what events have since shown—that France was not fitted for republican institutions. By his

4

resolute adherence to the policy which prudence and patriotism dictated, the United States were saved from embroilment in the European difficulties. But the French Minister, and indeed the French Government, took the highly indelicate and aggressive attitude of appeals to the prejudices of the American people against the government; the Minister setting on foot expeditions, in defiance of law, against England and Spain; and successive ministers addressing letters to the government, which in more than one case were published simultaneously with their presentation to the authorities. These were often written in a spirit of arrogance and insult which it is difficult now to conceive possible. They were issued at periods when they might have an influence on elections; and when the choice of a successor to General Washington was pending, one of these offensive documents made its appearance. And not only were these acknowledged papers put forth, but through the press appeared unacknowledged articles, written by the same dictation.

General Washington, after eight years' service, was succeeded by John Adams, in 1797. Notwithstanding the efforts of his opposers, foreign and domestic, such was the moral grandeur of his character, that Washington might have received a third unanimous election. But he declined a re-election in the Farewell Address, which has ever since been appealed to as defining American policy; and which even the eloquence of Kossuth, during his late tour, could not set aside, or persuade the nation to forget. Thus has experience vindicated the wisdom of Washington, although some of his contemporaries, and among them patriots and well-wishers to their country, second only to himself in fame, differed from him in opinion.

His successor had not the prestige of a name so honored to second his administration. At that time, the mode of election differed from the present. Each elector deposited two names, without designating either as President or Vice-President. The candidate who had the highest vote was declared President, and the next in order Vice-President. Thus Mr. Adams had for his Vice-President, Mr. Jefferson, who was pledged to a different line of policy from that which Mr. A. pursued. The practical difficulties which this mode of election caused were perceived, and the present method of electing President and Vice-President has been substituted.

Without the unanimity of choice which elected Washington, and laboring under the disadvantage of having received a partisan vote, being elected over Mr. Jefferson by a majority of three only, Mr. Adams had great difficulties to contend with. The French Government became even more aggressive than under Washington's administration, and the British Government did nothing which could reconcile the people to what was represented as the undue partiality of the administration for that power. Affairs reached such a crisis that war with France was deemed inevitable, and General Washington was summoned from his retirement to take command of the American army. The subject was thus introduced, by President Adams, to the attention of Washington : "In forming an army, whenever I must come to that extremity, I am at an immense loss whether to call out the old generals, or to appoint a new set. If the French come here, we must learn to march with a quick step, and to attack, for in that way only they are said to be vulnerable. I must tax you sometimes for advice. We must have your name, if you will in any case permit us to use it. There will be more efficacy in it, than in many an army."

The difficulty did not, however, proceed to open war, being averted by negotiation. Much was endured. Spoliations on American commerce took place, and the flag of the United States was insulted by both England and France. But the conduct of the latter power was most preposterous, particularly to the American envoys who were sent to Paris to negotiate. These envoys were even menaced in France with odium in America, which the French authorities threatened to excite against them. When these facts were officially published, an universal feeling of indignation in the United States overcame all party prejudice, and as the French authorities demanded money as a preliminary condition to any negotiations, the answer of the American people was " millions for defence, not a cent for tribute !"* Under the pressure of these causes, and while the United States seemed to be contemptuously treated as an instrument in the hands of foreign nations—neither Great Britain nor France fully acknowledging her independence — the famous Alien and Sedition Acts were passed. Great Britain continued to hold forts on our Western frontier, and within our acknowledged

---

* Marshall.

4*

territories, and insisted on her claim to search
our vessels, and impress men alleged to be her
subjects. France, in the manner already described, tacitly denied our nationality; and both
nations seemed to have forgotten that the United
States had ceased to be British provinces, and
were therefore no longer a mere battle-ground
for European quarrels. By the Alion Act, the
President of the United States was authorized to
send aliens—as foreigners are termed—out of the
United States, if he deemed them dangerous
characters; and no form of judicial proceeding
was necessary in the case. And by the Sedition
Act, prosecutions could be maintained against
those parties who accused the government un-
justly.

CHAPTER IV.

DEMOCRATS AND FEDERALISTS — MR. CLAY TAKES THE
FIELD AGAINST THE ALIEN AND SEDITION ACTS — MR.
CLAY AND EMANCIPATION—IS APPOINTED U. S. SENATOR
—"OLD BESS."

GENERAL LAFAYETTE well pronounced the Constitution of the United States "a happy compound of State rights and Federal energy." But the precise limits of the Federal and State sovereignties it was impossible to state in any instrument written by man. The trial of the compact by circumstances must define its nature; and it was Henry Clay's privilege to be, in youth, the attentive observer of the progress of the events which have determined many important questions. Chancellor Wythe, his early friend, was one of the framers of the Constitution; and the proper ambition of the young man brought him in contact with many other of the leading spirits of the day. There were two great contending parties; the Federalists — who were accused of the intention to strengthen the United States Government at the expense of the rights of the States; and the Democrats—who were for leaving the largest latitude to the States, to guard against disunion. The councils of the former party prevailed during the days of Washington; but the moderation of that magistrate, and the democratic tendencies of the people, prevented any such evil as was apprehended. On the other hand, the reaction caused by the disastrous issue of the French attempt at a republic, checked democracy from exceeding the limits of safety; and between the struggles of the two parties, rules were established which have settled the policy of the United States down to the present day. There are still many questions which remain undecided, but as none of them equal in importance what have already been determined, we need not doubt that the Federal Union will prove strong enough for any exigence. When Jefferson came into power, he declared the contest upon the original disputes of the two great parties, at an end. " We are all republicans — we are all federalists."

To return to the subject of our narrative — Henry Clay. The matter introduced at the close of the last chapter, is necessary as preliminary to noticing young Clay's first appearance as a politician. It was at the early age of twenty-one, as an earnest opponent of the Alien and Sedition Laws. Great as was the excitement which followed upon these enactments, they passed Congress without any very strenuous opposition. Once enacted, however, they were the rallying point of the opposition. To give the President absolute and unquestioned power over the liberties even of foreigners, and to restrain the liberty of the press in the discussion of the acts of the public servants, were regarded as dangerous steps, tending to monarchy and absolutism. The legislatures of Virginia and Kentucky passed strong resolutions condemning these laws as unconstitutional, and calling upon the other States for responses. But the then existing evil of foreign interference—"the intrigues of foreign emissaries, employed by the profligate government of the French Directory, who abused the freedom of the press by traducing the character of the administration and its friends, and by instigating the resistance of the people against the government and laws of the Union"*—this evil, we say, was so much more apparent than the theoretical regal

---

* J. Q. Adams.

danger, that none other of the States joined with Kentucky and Virginia, and several strongly disapproved of their resolutions. But both measures proved so decidedly unpopular, that nothing like them has ever been repeated. The Alien Law expired, by its own limitation, in 1800, and the Sedition Law in 1801. Perhaps, with the eminent statesman already quoted, we may safely pronounce the acts themselves, and the resolutions concerning them, as adversary party measures.

Mr. Clay appeared in the field as the earnest opposer of these laws. No reports of his early speeches on any subject are preserved, and we have not met even a sketch of his highly popular harangues upon this subject. It would be curious to know to what length the ardent young politician proceeded; particularly as the legislature of Kentucky, in her resolutions, affirmed the right of nullification as the proper remedy for unconstitutional acts of the Federal Government. But in the absence of a full report, it would be highly unjust to hold the popular orator responsible for all the measures taken by those whose election he advocated.

Young politicians are ardent, and usually unselfish—or less selfish than older men. No doubt many a man has unconsciously defended what he esteemed the right with the more zeal that it chanced to be popular, and that it thus opened a path for his ambition. Still, the younger men in a republic look more to patriotic and high national considerations, than to expediency; for expediency must make, more or less, an important element in a veteran politician's calculations. We may therefore concede to young Clay the merit of discerning what subsequent events have proved, that the power of banishing even aliens simply upon the suspicion of the Executive, is not a prerogative which comports with the genius of our institutions.

Whatever desire of popularity may have entered into Mr. Clay's course upon the Alien and Sedition Laws, there was another subject on which he did not hesitate to defend the unpopular side, deeming it the right. A convention was about assembling to prepare a Constitution for Kentucky, and Henry Clay was one of the earnest advocates of a provision for the gradual abolition of slavery in the Commonwealth. The measure failed, the majority of the people out-voting the emancipationists. Mr. Clay had, previously to his public and personal advocacy of this reform, strongly urged it in a series of papers published in the Kentucky Gazette. Frequent reference has been made by Mr. Clay to this period in his life. We subjoin an extract from a speech delivered by him at the anniversary meeting of the Kentucky Colonization Society, at Frankfort, in 1829 : —

"More than thirty years ago, an attempt was made in this Commonwealth to adopt a system of gradual emancipation, similar to that introduced in Pennsylvania, in 1780. And among the acts of my life which I look back to with most satisfaction, is that of my having co-operated with zealous and intelligent friends to procure the establishment of that system in this State. We believed that the sum of good which would be attained by the State of Kentucky, in a gradual emancipation of her slaves, would far transcend the aggregate of mischief which might result to herself and the Union together, from the gradual liberation of them, and their dispersion and residence in the United States. We were overpowered by numbers, but submitted to the decision of the majority, with a grace which the minority, in a republic, should ever yield to such a decision. I have nevertheless never ceased, and never shall cease to regret a decision, the effects of which have been to place us in the rear of our neighbors, who are exempt from slavery, in the state of agriculture, the progress of manufactures, the advance of improvements, and the general prosperity of society."

It will be sufficient to add, in this connection, that Mr. Clay's disposal of his slave property, by will, shows that he retained to the last his ideas upon gradual emancipation, and that he remained during his life a friend to the Colonization enterprise. His public labors and speeches, in early life, had the effect to secure a reputation which brought him many and profitable clients. Both as a civil, and as a criminal lawyer, he was soon highly distinguished; and it is said that no alleged criminal whose defence he undertook, failed to obtain discharge or acquittal.

In 1803, Mr. Clay was elected to the legislature of his adopted State. Matters of local interest caused him to be selected, but the election was a high compliment to his talents and legal learning. The Lexington Insurance Company was menaced with a repeal of its charter, and the late Hon. Felix Grundy was an advocate of the measure. Mr. Clay was opposed to it; and both gentlemen had been employed as counsel by the parties, whose controversy brought the question to an issue. In the House the question came up, and was debated with much pertinacity and ability. The House decided against the corporation; but the Senators, who had many of them been present, reversed this decision. Mr. Clay's short service in the State Legislature was followed by his appointment by the Executive of the State to complete, in the United States Senate, the term of General Adair, who had resigned.

Whatever may be charged against the unfortunate and erring Aaron Burr, no one will suspect him of any deficiency in legal acumen. It was, therefore, a great compliment to Henry Clay, that upon two occasions when Burr was arrested in Kentucky, he applied to young Clay as his counsel. In neither case was a bill of indictment found against Burr, who was subsequently arrested, and tried on various charges of treason and misdemeanor. What the man intended to do, still remains a mystery. The difficulty which we have seen in our own day, attending the trial of persons charged with organising military expeditions in the United States, and the sympathy which is always enlisted in behalf of those who are prosecuted for political offences of this nature, will account for Mr. Clay's undertaking the defence of Burr. It is proper to observe, however, that as the developments of the trial proved Burr to have deceived him, Mr. Clay regretted that he had ever listened to his request. But in befriending Colonel Burr, he only shared the common feeling of the people of generous Kentucky. Mr. Clay did not appear in the trial of Colonel Burr at Richmond, nor in that trial was Burr convicted; though the verdict of popular opinion was passed against him, from which he never recovered.

Mr. Clay's appointment to Congress, in 1806, was but for a single session of the Senate. Even in that brief period, he gave earnest of his future fame and influence. At that early day in the history of our national legislation, no congressional act was unimportant; parties and statesmen narrowly watched each other, since votes on subjects which would now be regarded as unimportant, then had a signification as fixing the practice of the government. The subject of debate when Mr. Clay took his seat in the Senate in 1806, was the erection of a bridge over the Potomac at the expense of the United States

Government. The principle involved was the constitutionality of public improvements at the government expense. Mr. Clay here commenced the course which he uniformly followed — the defence of that policy — and his speech is represented as one of the best he has delivered.

In 1807, Mr. Clay's Congressional term having expired, he was again elected to the Legislature of Kentucky. To his early "canvassing" the following anecdote is referred. Mr. Clay was addressing a crowd, when a party of riflemen, who had been practising, drew near to listen. They were pleased with the off-hand and attractive style of his oratory, but, backwoodsmen-like, considered that there were other requisites to manhood, beside the capacity to talk. They wanted no representative who was not able to honor the Kentucky weapon, and do good service with the rifle. An old man in the company, who seemed to have the place of "spokesman" assigned to him, beckoned to Mr. Clay to come towards him, when his speech was finished. A candidate for office, who is soliciting the popular suffrage, must be very courteous; so he obeyed the signal.

"Young man," said the Nimrod, "you want to go to the Legislature?"

Mr. Clay acknowledged this — very modestly of course—principally on account of his friends; though he confessed, having been nominated, he should like to be successful. But he was hardly prepared for the next question.

"Are you a good shot?"

Now shooting has little to do with legislation, but a great deal depended upon the favor of these marksmen. We are afraid that Mr. Clay had some mental reservation behind the reply that "he *considered himself* a good marksman!" But he was to be proved.

"Then you shall go to the Legislature," said Nimrod; "but we must see you shoot!"

There was no escape. Mr. Clay pleaded that his own rifle was at home, and he never shot with any other.

"No matter," said the hunter. "Here's *Old Bess;* she never fails in the hands of a hunter. She has put a bullet through many a squirrel's head, at a hundred yards. If you can shoot with anything, you can with *Old Bess.*"

"Very well!" said Mr. Clay, "put up your mark." There was no escape, and he was resolved to try, "hit or miss." The target was placed at eighty yards, and Mr. Clay, bringing the piece to his shoulder, pierced the centre — very much, we suspect, to his own astonishment.

"A chance shot!" cried his political opponents. "He can't do it again in a hundred times trying. Let him try it over!"

"Beat *that*, and I will!" said Mr. Clay. It was a fair offer, but no one accepted it; and he, leaving well enough alone, passed with the crowd as a good marksman. He had moreover, in after life, more fame in rifle practice than he desired. When in Europe, as commissioner to make a treaty with England, at the close of the war of 1812, he was represented in an English paper as the man who killed Tecumseh; and furthermore, it was stated with all gravity, caused several razor strops to be made from the fallen Indian's skin!

While relating anecdotes, we may mention another which Mr. Clay used to relate with much humor. He was once opposed to a gentleman who had but one arm, and an Irish wag who was under obligations to him, voted for his opponent on the plea that he chose the man who could put but *one hand* into the public treasury.

CHAPTER V.

MR. CLAY IN THE KENTUCKY LEGISLATURE -- DIFFICULTY
WITH MR. MARSHALL — AGAIN SENT TO THE SENATE —
MR. CLAY UPON "PROTECTION"—GOVERNOR SHELBY—
THE GOVERNOR'S HOUSEHOLD—MR. CLAY'S HOUSEHOLD
— ASHLAND — THE BOTTLE OF WINE.

IN the Legislature of Kentucky, in 1808, Mr.
Clay introduced a resolution to the effect that the
members, to encourage domestic manufactures,
and to give their constituents an example, should
clothe themselves in fabrics of domestic manufacture. It was always a favorite opinion with some
of the prominent legislators and statesmen of our
republic, that domestic manufactures should be
encouraged by the exclusion of foreign, or by such
taxes on foreign goods as would give American
the preference in cheapness. Others have resisted
the policy of "protection," as it is termed, desiring
to leave foreign and domestic fabrics to stand
upon the ground of unfettered competition. The
right of the government of the United States to

impose duties of a prohibitory, or even "protective" character, has been denied by many.

War, viewed in whatever light we choose, is a great evil; and when, according to the rule of national custom or intercourse, it becomes necessary to resist aggression, or to assert right, the advantages which may be secured through the successful prosecution of warfare, are always heavily balanced by the misfortunes and social disadvantages which result from even a victorious struggle. We have noticed in preceding chapters the bitterness which the remains of the war feeling caused in the early councils of our country, and the charge of favor for one nation, and enmity against another, which were mutually alleged against the great parties in the United States. The protective policy was defended and attacked on similar grounds. It was the policy of Great Britain to discourage, and prevent manufactures in her colonies, in order to make them dependent upon the mother country. This system was carried to such an oppressive length, that it formed one of the most serious subjects of complaint in the colonies against Great Britain, and was among the causes which led to the war of the Revolution.

When the United States became independent of Great Britain, it was obvious that the inde pendence was nominal only, while we were dependent upon a foreign nation for articles necessary not only for government purposes, but for the daily uses of life. All admitted this; the question was whether American manufactures should be left to struggle, unaided, against foreign rivalry, or whether legislative enactments should assist the American against the foreign article. Mr. Clay was an earnest supporter of the latter opinion. With such views, he brought forward the resolution spoken of above. It was a stormy session of the legislature, many subjects of importance being canvassed, and no little heat being exhibited. Out of this exciting state of things grew a personal difficulty, which resulted in a duel between Mr. Clay and Humphrey Marshall. We should be glad if there were no such passage as this to record in his life; but it is no faithful performance of the duty of a biographer, to suppress the account of the faults of the subject of his work. Duelling is an indefensible practice, and no man has more strongly condemned it than Mr. Clay himself. He said, in an address to his constituents, in 1825,—" I owe it to the commu nity to say, that whatever heretofore I may have done, or by inevitable circumstances might be forced to do, no man holds in deeper abhorrence than I do, this pernicious practice. Condemned, as it must be, by the judgment and philosophy— to say nothing of the religion—of every thinking man, it is an affair of feeling about which we cannot, though we should, reason. Its true corrective will be found when all shall unite, as all ought to unite, in its unqualified proscription." Mr. Clay's abhorrence of duelling is just — his apology is weak. The same sophistry would apply to any act of violence, of revenge, or of slavish conformity to the false opinions of the world. What judgment, philosophy, and religion condemn, cannot be defended; nor can *necessity* be pleaded for it. True courage sets at defiance the sneers of a world which urge a man to do evil. There is no heroism in preferring the chance of a pistol-shot—the danger of murdering or being murdered—to the terror of a false public opinion. And this erroneous estimate of honor is one of the teachings of war. Yet there have been warriors who refused, upon principle, to engage in a duel; as there have also been, and still are, many civilians who aspire to the reputation of submitting their quarrels to the false arbitration of the duel.

Mr. Clay's meeting with Marshall resulted in no fatal consequences. He was spared the remorse of murder, and his own life was reserved for the long line of public service to which we now return. He was again elected, in 1809, to fill another Senatorial vacancy, that was created by the resignation of the Hon. Bucknor Thurston. During this session of Congress, he took occasion to bring forward an amendment embodying his views of the protection of domestic industry. A bill was under discussion to purchase cordage, sail-cloth, and other munitions of war; and to this an amendment was moved, that preference should be given, in the purchase, to articles of domestic manufacture. The sole object considered in the tariff, up to this date, was the provision of revenue for governmental expenses. But Mr. Clay, with other statesmen, saw the necessity of the provision within ourselves of the necessaries which war, by interrupting commerce, might cut off. Washington and Jefferson had distinctly recommended the fostering of domestic industry; and Madison, then President, had urged upon Congress such alterations in the laws, as should more especially protect and foster the several branches of manufacture which had then been commenced. The bill above mentioned, with the amendment, was carried by a large majority. We subjoin an extract from Mr. Clay's speech :—

"It is a subject no less of curiosity than of interest to trace the prejudices in favor of foreign fabrics. In our colonial condition, we were in a complete state of dependence on the mother country, as it respected manufactures as well as commerce. For many years after the war, such was the partiality for her productions in this country, that a gentleman's head could not withstand the influence of solar heat, unless covered with a London hat; his feet could not bear the pebbles or frost, unless protected by London shoes; and the comfort or ornament of his person was only consulted, when his coat was cut by the shears of a tailor 'just from London!' At length, however, the wonderful discovery has been made, that it is not absolutely beyond the reach of American skill and ingenuity, to produce these articles, combining with equal elegance greater durability. And I entertain no doubt, that in a short time the no less important fact will be developed, that the domestic manufactures of the

United States, fostered by government, and aided by household exertions, are fully competent to supply us with at least every necessary article of clothing. I therefore, Sir, am in favor of encouraging them, not to the extent to which they are carried in England, but to such an extent as will redeem us entirely from all dependence on foreign countries. There is a pleasure—a pride, if I may be allowed the expression—(and I pity those who cannot feel the sentiment) in being clad in the productions of our own families. Others may prefer the cloths of Leeds and of London, but give me those of Humphreysville."

From a speech delivered at a later date, we make the following extract. We may premise that the man here held up as a model, was one of those men of the revolutionary era, of whose friendship Henry Clay was justly proud, and whose experience and advice aided in forming his character. Governor Shelby commenced his service of his country in the Indian wars prior to the declaration of independence. He served through the whole revolutionary war in the field, and as a legislator, as soldier, surveyor, and commissary; giving evidence of prudence, scientific knowledge, and bravery, which entitle him to

6

high distinction, and also to solid reputation. He was a member of the convention which formed the Constitution of Kentucky, and was chosen the first governor of that State. He was again elected governor in 1812, and at his advanced age, was active in the second war with Great Britain, marching with four thousand men to the frontier where General Harrison commanded. After the close of his gubernatorial term, he held several important trusts, till overtaken by the infirmities of age. He died in 1826, at the age of seventy-six years. Such was the man whom Henry Clay thus cites as an example:—

"If you want to find an example of order, of freedom from debt, of economy, of expenditure falling below, rather than exceeding income, you will go to the well-regulated family of a farmer. You will go to the house of such a man as Isaac Shelby. You will not find him haunting taverns, engaged in broils, prosecuting angry lawsuits; you will behold every member of his family clad with the produce of their own hands, and usefully employed — the spinning-wheel and the loom in motion by day-break. With what pleasure will his wife carry you into her neat dairy, lead you into her store-house, and point you to the tablecloths, the sheets,. the counterpanes, which lie on this shelf for one daughter, or on that for another, all prepared in advance by her provident care, for the day of their respective marriages. If you want to see an opposite example, go to the house of a man who manufactures nothing at home, whose family resort to the store for everything they consume. You will find him, perhaps, at the tavern, or at the shop at the cross-roads. He is engaged, with the rum-grog on the table, taking depositions to make out some case of usury or fraud. Or perhaps he is furnishing to his lawyer the materials to prepare a long bill of injunction in some intricate case. The sheriff is hovering about his farm to serve some new writ. On court days—he never misses attending them—you will find him eagerly collecting his witnesses to defend himself against the merchant's and the doctor's claims. Go to his house, and after the short and giddy period that his daughters have flirted about the country in their calico and muslin frocks, what a scene of discomfort and distress is presented to you there! What the individual family of Isaac Shelby is, I wish to see the nation, in the aggregate, become. * * * If statesmen would carefully observe the conduct of private individuals in the management of their own affairs, they would have much surer guides in promoting the interests of the state, than the visionary speculations of theoretical writers."

Having copied Mr. Clay's picture of the house hold of Governor Shelby, it will not be out of place to introduce here the domestic establishment of Mr. Clay, as described by one of his biographers.* At the date of Mr. Clay's appointment to the Senate, in 1809, he had been married ten years. Commencing life as a professional and public man at a very early age, it was fortunate for him, perhaps, that he had thus early also the responsibilities of the head of a household. His wife, who survives him, was born in Hagerstown, Maryland, in 1781, being thus four years younger than her husband. Her father was Colonel Thomas Hart, a gentleman of high standing in Lexington; for whom Mr. Clay's respect, and Mrs. Clay's affection, is shown by their giving the mother's paternal name to several of their children. The date of the following extract was 1842 :—

"Mr. Clay, in all his domestic relations, has sustained through life an exemplary and spotless

---

* Colton.

ASHLAND, THE RESIDENCE OF MR. CLAY.

reputation as a husband, father, and master. During his long public career, himself the observed of all observers, few away from Lexington and the neighborhood ever heard any thing of his family, simply because everything there was as it should be. It has been a quiet history, because it has been without fault, and without ostentation. The virtues of Mrs. Clay, as a faithful wife, an affectionate mother, and a kind mistress, have not been altogether unknown. At the head of a great household, her cares, in the absence of her husband on public duty, so frequent, and often long protracted, have necessarily been habitually extended to interests out of doors, as well as to the customary domain of woman; and no lady was ever better qualified for the position she has so long occupied. Her dairy, garden, the pleasure grounds of Ashland — all on a large scale — and her green-house, were always supervised by her; and the operations of a farm of between five and six hundred acres, were not less constantly somewhat under her care. The feeding and clothing of all the men and women on the farm and in the house, being some fifty or sixty in all, also required her attention, together with caring for the sick. Not a gallon of milk, nor a pound of

6*

butter, nor any of the garden vegetables, went to market without her personal supervision; and the extent of these duties may be partly imagined from the fact, that the Phœnix Hotel, in Lexington, is supplied with thirty gallons of milk per day from Ashland, in the summer, and twenty in the winter. Mrs. Clay is the first up in the morning, and the last to bed at night. When General Bertrand was a guest at Ashland, he was much astonished at the extent and variety of duties discharged by Mrs. Clay, and at the activity and system with which they were accomplished. The servants, in door and out, cared for in health and in sickness, in infancy and in old age, well-housed, well-clad, well-fed, exempt from the anxieties of life, and always treated with indulgence, would never have known they were in a state of bondage, if they had not been told."

The reader will not, we presume, be displeased to learn something more of Ashland. We extract from the same source as the above, the following brief and interesting description: "Ashland, comprising the house, gardens, and park, is situated a mile and a half south-east from the court house in Lexington. The whole estate consists of between five and six hundred acres of the best land in Kentucky, which, for agricultural purposes, is one of the richest States in the Union. Ashland proper was projected for an elegant country-seat. The house is a spacious brick mansion, without much pretension in architecture, surrounded by lawns and pleasure-grounds, interspersed with walks and groves, planted with almost every variety of American shrubbery and forest trees, executed under the direction of Mr. and Mrs. Clay. Mr. Clay appears to have delighted in gathering around him the plants and trees of his own country, there being among them few exotics. As the domicil of the great American statesman, Ashland is one of the household words of the American people. Having been deeply lodged in their affections, so long as the memory of the great proprietor is cherished, it cannot fail to have a place in history."

And, we may add, it is an evidence of what energy and talent—talent not ashamed of industry—may accomplish for a young American. He who finds a model in such a man as Isaac Shelby, cannot fail to become independent of debt — except, indeed, when drawn into embarrassment by misfortune. Mr. Clay has been twice seriously embarrassed — but in both instances by liabilities for others. . His manner of living was without ostentation, and his habit has been to make no engagements which he could not promptly meet. But we must not anticipate our narrative.

An amusing anecdote is related of Mr. Clay in connection with his defence of American manufactures and productions. A western vine-grower presented him with some specimen bottles of American wine. So pleased was he with this evidence that we need not go abroad even for luxuries, that at his annual visit to Washington, he carried a bottle or two with him, to astonish the anti-American-system men, with the American vintage. It was produced by him at a public table, duly prefaced with a brief "protective speech." Upon tasting it, his guests, in spite of their politeness, looked awry and astonished indeed. Mr. Clay hasted to put it to his own lips, and found it was — very respectable whiskey! Subsequent inquiry developed the fact that some of his servants with an epicurean taste, had drunk the wine, and, fearing detection, refilled the bottles with something decidedly American to be sure—but still quite *foreign* to the purpose.

CHAPTER VI.

NAVIGATION OF THE MISSISSIPPI — LOUISIANA CEDED TO
FRANCE BY SPAIN—NAPOLEON'S PROJECT OF A MILITARY
COLONY — HIS DOUBLE PERFIDY TO THE UNITED STATES
AND SPAIN — PURCHASE OF LOUISIANA BY THE UNITED
STATES—DISPUTED BOUNDARY OF FLORIDA—MEASURES
OF MR. MADISON IN RELATION THERETO—SUSTAINED BY
MR. CLAY.

AMONG the less familiar passages of history, is
the fact that this continent narrowly escaped
being made the theatre of the exercise of the
warlike spirit of Napoleon Bonaparte. Louisiana
was ceded to Spain by France in 1763, and remained in Spanish occupation until 1800. Florida
was also a Spanish possession, having been restored
to that power in 1783, after twenty years' nominal
occupation by England. Thus the whole of the
southern and western border of the United States
was in the possession of Spain. After much
negotiation, and many lowering indications of
difficulty, the United States obtained from Spain,

by treaty, the right to navigate the Mississippi, and also the privilege of using the city of New Orleans as a place of deposit.

In 1800, Napoleon compelled Spain to re-cede Louisiana to France, in the treaty of retrocession binding himself not to suffer the colony to go into the hands of the United States. But, as he did not wish to have the possession of Louisiana clogged by any conditions, he compelled Spain to annul or withdraw the treaty stipulation by which the United States enjoyed the use of the waters of the Mississippi. Florida still remained in the hands of Spain, and the boundary between Florida and Louisiana was not very accurately defined by the treaty of retrocession. Napoleon was not unwilling, probably, to have open questions both with the United States and with Spain; for a new scene of operations was open, before his mind, on this continent, and occasions of dispute would further his designs.

The transfer of Louisiana to France had been stipulated, but not made public. The designs of Napoleon, whatever they may have been, were studiously concealed; but the temper of the French Government toward the United States, was anything but conciliatory. An armament was prepared to take possession of the newly-acquired province, and twenty thousand troops waited embarkation at Helvoetsluys, under the command of Bernadotte. That the destination of this force was for America, we have the official declaration of the French Government. The war between England and France had ceased, by the treaty of Amiens, in 1801; but the details of the treaty remained unfulfilled, and were the subject of continual anger and bitterness. England regarded with jealousy every movement of France, and although Napoleon insisted to the day of his death, that he intended at that juncture no enterprise against Britain, yet the movements of the French troops in the ports of France and Holland were made the occasion of hostile preparations in England. A note by Talleyrand, handed to the British Ambassador in answer to a royal address to the British Parliament, distinctly said: "If His Britannic Majesty, in his message, means to speak of the expedition of Helvoetsluys, all the world knows that it was destined for America, and was on the point of sailing; but in consequence of that message, its orders are counter manded."

What a succession of quarrels, difficulties, and

wars, must have followed the attempt to control the Mississippi, and hold the western part of this continent! "Louisiana" had a meaning almost indefinite; and the power to annoy which such an occupation would have given France, might have been full of great and unhappy results. Not the least of these, would have been the compulsion of the United States into European war; the continuation of our colonial misfortunes.

The spirited language of a great American statesman and orator* thus describes the aim of Napoleon: "Here it had been his purpose to establish a military colony, with the Mexican dominions of Spain on one side, and the United States of America and the continental colonies of Great Britain on the other, in the centre of the western hemisphere — the stand for a lever to wield at his pleasure the destinies of the world. * * * The restless spirit of Napoleon, inflamed at the age of most active energy in human life, by the gain of fifty battles, dazzling with a splendor then unrivalled but by the renown of Cæsar, breathing for a moment in the midway path of his career, the conqueror of Egypt—the victor of Lodi and Marengo — the trampler upon the neck

---

* J. Q. Adams.

of his country, her people, her legislators, and her constitution — was about to bring his veteran legions in formidable proximity to this Union. * * * In re-purchasing from Spain the colony of Louisiana, Napoleon — to hold in his hand a rod over the western section of the United States —had compelled the dastardly and imbecile monarch of Spain to commit an act of perfidy, by withdrawing from the people of the United States the stipulated right of deposit at New Orleans. The great artery of the commerce of the Union was thus checked in its circulation. The sentiment of surprise, of alarm, of indignation, was universal among the people. The hardy and enterprising settlers of the western country could hardly be restrained from pouring down the swelling floods of their population, to take possession of New Orleans itself, by the rights of war."

Even in Congress there were indications of a war-spirit. To meet the dilemma, President Jefferson sent Mr. Monroe to France, to be joined in a Commission Extraordinary with R. H. Livingston, then Resident American Minister in Paris. Their commission was to purchase the island of New Orleans, and the Spanish territory

7

east of the Mississippi. Mr. Monroe had scarcely reached Paris, when he and his colleague were informed of the readiness of the French Government to cede to the United States the whole of Louisiana. Napoleon had too much work on his hands already, in the threatened renewal of the war with Great Britain, to cumber himself with an American colony, which would offer a new point of attack for his European enemies, and entangle him, also, in a contest with the United States. He needed money, and could spare no troops for trans-atlantic operations. To accept the proposition to take the whole colony of Louisiana, exceeded the powers of the commissioners, and the funds at their disposal. But they closed with the offer, and in a few months, the "Great West" became, by treaty, a portion of the domain of the United States.

Spain objected to the violation of Napoleon's compact. The cession to the United States was directly contrary to his promise. He silenced Spain, so far as the cession was concerned; but there still remained an unsettled question. What was the eastern boundary of Louisiana? Spain deemed that it included anything this side of the Mississippi, and Napoleon's government defended her in the assumption. And yet it is said that he was prepared to claim and occupy to the river Perdido, the present western boundary of Florida. The French Commissioner to take possession of the colony for France, admitted this fact to a member of the United States Senate, as that gentleman declared on the floor of the Senate chamber.

Thus the matter remained in dispute until 1810. Congress passed laws at a much earlier period, asserting the sovereignty of the United States over the disputed territory, but they were not uniformly enforced, until, in the year above mentioned, President Madison issued a proclamation, and in pursuance of it, occupied the disputed ground.

During Mr. Clay's second term of service as Senator, the act of Mr. Madison, in asserting jurisdiction east of the Mississippi, was the subject of debate. Mr. Clay vindicated the measure, declaring that the President would have been criminally inattentive to his duty had he neglected to exercise the discretionary power vested in him by the Acts of Congress above referred to. He examined and stated the legal points of the matter at issue between the United States and

Spain with the acuteness of a lawyer, and pressed the vindication of American honor with the warmth of a patriot. He demonstrated the necessity, to the United States, of the possession of the whole of Florida. He ridiculed the fear of foreign interference to protect Spain in her demands, and closed with the hope of seeing the United States embrace the whole country east of the Mississippi. None knew better than he the rights of this nation; and none more warmly resisted the pretence of European powers to retain unoccupied tracts on the continent, for the purpose of cession and retrocession in adjusting treaty balances. Mr. Madison was sustained by Congress in the step he had taken.

CHAPTER VII.

THE BANK OF THE UNITED STATES—MR. CLAY IN 1811— COW AND TURKEY — MR. CLAY IN 1816.

THE first Bank of the United States was chartered by Act of Congress, in 1791, for the term of twenty years. We have not space, within our limits, to discuss at length the subject of Banks and Banking, and shall allude to it only so far as necessary to explain Mr. Clay's connection with it. And even that reference must be brief, since it will prove less interesting to our readers than any other portion of his life; and, we may add, in such a work as this, less instructive.

In 1811, came up the question of the re-charter of the Bank. No human institutions can be perfect; and while representative governments have high advantages over all others, there are certainly some respects in which they do not work to advantage. Banks dependent upon popular legislation for re-charter or continuance, are frequently liable to depreciation of credit.

7*

Such institutions should be not only above mercantile reproach, but above suspicion; as fluctuations in the value of their stock and notes, occasion public losses to the advantage of speculators and stock operators.

Availing ourselves of the labors of a distinguished writer on the subject,* we condense from his summary view an abstract of the arguments by which the first Bank was defended. These were, the credit and value it would impart to government stocks; the convenience to the treasury in the collection and disbursement of the revenue of the government; and the facilities it would afford to merchants and others. On the other hand, the opponents of the proposed Bank alleged that banking institutions were artful contrivances of cunning men to grow rich at the expense of the people; that the Bank would tend to strengthen the hands of the Executive, already too strong; and that the charter was unconstitutional. The Bank was created by a very close vote, the democratic party going against it. It proved all that it promised in reference to raising the value of government securities, United States Stock being taken as

---

* Hildreth, on Banks and Banking.

payment. The advantages which it afforded to the Treasury Department were evident, and its utility in that respect was great.

But the objection that the institution would strengthen the Executive, was not without its proof in the trial. The first Bank became, from the force of circumstances, a party institution. It had been sustained by the friends of Hamilton, and opposed by the friends of Jefferson; and when, in 1811, the question of the re-charter came up, it was defeated by one vote in the Senate, having passed the House. The Senate vote was a tie, and the Vice President's vote decided the fate of the application. Mr. Clay made, against the Bank, one of his most effective speeches, from the echo of which he has never been able to escape. Mr. Clay gave to his constituents, in 1816, three reasons for his opposition in 1811: first, that he was instructed by the Legislature to oppose the re-charter; second, that he believed the corporation had, during a portion of the period of its existence, abused its power, and had sought to subserve the views of a political party; and third, that as the power to create a corporation, such as was proposed to be continued, was not specifically granted in the

Constitution, and as the bank did not then appear to him to be necessary to carry into effect any of the powers which were specifically granted, Congress was not authorised to continue it. To relieve the dulness of this topic a little, it may be well to repeat an amusing passage from Mr. Clay's speech against the Bank, in 1811:

"A bank is made for the ostensible purpose of the collection of the revenue; and while it is engaged in this, the most inferior and subordinate of all its functions, it is made to diffuse itself throughout society, and to influence all the great operations of credit, circulation, and commerce. Like the Virginia justice, you tell the man whose turkey had been stolen, that your books of precedent furnish no form for his case, but that you will grant him a precept to search for a cow, and when looking for that he may possibly find his turkey! You say to this corporation, we cannot authorise you to discount, to emit paper, to regulate commerce, &c. No, our book has no precedent of that kind. But then we can authorise you to collect the revenue, and while occupied with that, you may do whatever else you please!"

In 1816, upon the suggestion of President Madison, the second Bank of the United States was chartered. Mr. Madison spake and voted against the charter of the first Bank in 1791, and indeed was active in opposition to the financial measures of Hamilton generally. Mr. Clay was one of the supporters of the new Bank, and exerted himself in its favor. This inconsistency has often been charged against him; but if inconsistent, he was not alone; for the Bank chartered in 1816 was established by the votes of those who had been the most strenuous in their opposition to the re-charter of the first Bank. The argument was, that at this crisis it was necessary, and therefore constitutional.

We do not purpose to follow the subject further. The discussion, in which Mr. Clay took a very active part, was renewed under the administration of General Jackson, who vetoed a third bank charter. The Independent Treasury scheme of Mr. Van Buren, and the efforts to re-establish a Bank, under Mr. Tyler, kept up the controversy upon the currency for many years. It has now ceased. Mr. Webster declared, in one of his speeches, that a National Bank is "an obsolete idea;" and to the same conclusion all parties seem to have arrived at last. If a bank chartered by the United States is unconstitutional, except

6

when *necessary* to enable the government to carry on its operations, its unconstitutionality is established by nearly twenty years' experience; and no party will now be impolitic enough to undertake again to establish a National Bank.

The jealousy of the great political parties has really had more to do with the question than any thing else. The democrats refused to re-charter the first Bank, because it was in the hands of federalists, and was charged with having been made their instrument; and the federalists, actuated by a similar feeling, voted against the second Bank, because, as a democratic measure, it might become their ally. The third attempt was defeated — certainly in part, if not altogether — on party grounds; and the paper currency of the country is well relieved from the inconveniences of a connection with national politics. The two banks unquestionably rendered good service in their day, with all their disadvantages. Each, at the close of wars which had impoverished the national exchequer, aided in the establishment of the national credit; and each rendered other important services, in circumstances which will not again occur. For instance, the Bank of 1816 relieved the Treasury of the United States of thirteen millions of the notes of non-specie-paying banks. The country has gained in experience, and in the elements of true wealth. The first will forbid the renewal of the dangerous alliance of bank and state—dangerous not so much to the state as to the bank, and the pockets and business of the people — and the second will put banking upon its true basis, whether conducted under state or national charters, or followed as an individual and private business.

CHAPTER VIII.

MR. CLAY SPEAKER OF THE HOUSE OF REPRESENTATIVES — CAUSES OF WAR — WAR RESOLUTIONS — BILLS FROM THE SENATE — MR. CLAY'S SPEECH IN COMMITTEE — JOHN RANDOLPH, OF ROANOKE.

WE have seen Mr. Clay twice a member of the Congress of the United States as Senator, filling the unexpired terms of others. In 1811, he received the higher popular honour of an election to the House of Representatives.

President Madison had summoned Congress to meet a month earlier than usual, on account of the disturbed condition of our foreign relations. Mr. Clay appeared in his place on Monday, November 4th, and was at once elected Speaker of the House. He received seventy-five votes out of one hundred and twenty-eight. On taking the chair, he acknowledged the honor done him, briefly and pertinently as follows : —

"Gentlemen, — In coming to the station which you have done me the honor to assign me — an

HENRY CLAY THE STATESMAN,

honor for which you will be pleased to accept my thanks — I obey rather your commands than my inclination. I am sensible of the imperfections which I bring along with me, and a consciousness of these would deter me from attempting a discharge of the duties of the chair, did I not rely confidently on your generous support. Should the rare and delicate occasion present itself, when your Speaker should be called upon to check or control the wanderings or intemperance of debate, your justice will, I hope, ascribe to his interposition the motives only of public good, and a regard to the dignity of the House. And, in all instances be assured, gentlemen, that I shall with infinite pleasure, afford every facility in my power to the despatch of public business, in the most agreeable manner."

The position of Speaker of the House, always one of importance, was forty years ago of even greater consequence than now. As we have had before occasion to remark, the policy of the government, and the Congressional usages of the United States, were as yet undetermined; and it was Mr. Clay's delicate duty to decide on points where he could not appeal to past usage. We may observe in evidence of his impartiality, that

8

although he had frequent occasion to d.ffer from members, yet in no case during the term that he presided, was his decision reversed by appeal to the House. His election was an indication of the temper in which Congress had assembled, as regarded our foreign relations. The nation was exasperated to resistance against European en- croachments, and Mr. Clay was regarded as the champion of a decided, and, if need should arise, of a warlike policy. His occupation of the chair precluded him from the opportunity of making himself felt as an orator, except when the House was in "Committee of the Whole." On such occasions, the Speaker leaves the chair, and ap- points a temporary chairman of the committee.

The intention of submitting questions to the Committee of the Whole, is to allow greater latitude in debate. The resolutions and votes of the House in Committee, are not binding or final, until formally taken up in the House, after the rising of the Committee. Thus, subjects are discussed with more freedom. The Committee of the Whole has been not inaptly termed a "debating club;" and perhaps that is its best designation.

President Madison's Message, on the opening

of Congress, recommended placing the country in an attitude of defence and resistance to the aggressions of European powers, to which we have frequently referred in these pages. The conduct of Great Britain was particularly oppressive. In enforcing her claim to the right of search for her own subjects, her cruisers impressed seamen from American vessels to the number of several thousands. How many of these were really British subjects, and what proportion were natives of America, cannot be precisely stated; but it was urged by Americans that all, whether native or adopted citizens, who sailed under the American flag, were entitled to its protection. Impressment, and compulsory service in a man-of-war, is hard enough for those who acknowledge the sovereignty of a government which pursues such an oppressive policy; but when natives of another country, or those who have elected that other country for their future allegiance, are forcibly seized, such an outrage merits the appellation of "man-stealing," which was freely applied to it.

Another grievance was the proclamation by Great Britain, that all the ports of France were in a state of blockade, and the seizure of American vessels, any where upon the ocean, which were bound to French ports. A blockade, to be legal, must have a sufficient force to maintain it; a force stationed off the blockaded port, to arrest the vessels entering; but when the blockade is merely a proclamation, and vessels are seized wherever found, the act becomes one of war upon neutral powers.

Such were the leading causes of complaint against Great Britain. From similar acts of injustice, France was by no means free. The French Government interrupted our commerce nearly to as great an extent as Great Britain, only that France did not impress our seamen; and this violation of the personal rights and liberties of American citizens, was the popular ground of enmity to Great Britain. It excited a determination to resist; and it opened a path for young politicians to popular support and sympathy. Henry Clay was one of the acknowledged leaders of " Young America" at this period, and as such he was elected to Congress, and placed in the Speaker's chair of the House of Representatives. He was impetuous and daring — and in his early days carried his measures with a will as strong as his words were eloquent.

The Speaker has the appointment of standing

committees; and the Committee on Foreign
Relations, appointed by Mr. Clay, early reported.
The report represented that France had practically desisted from her encroachments on American commerce, while Great Britain still adhered
to her oppressive course, and the Committee
concluded with a series of appropriate resolutions.
These recommended the increase of the regular
army, the fitting out of all the national vessels,
the acceptance of the services of volunteers, and
permission to merchant vessels to arm in their
own defence. All these resolutions were carried
by large majorities, but not without warm debate.
The minority — at the head of whom stood the
able, though eccentric, John Randolph of Roanoke — combated these measures at every stage;
but, contrary to custom and precedent, the report
was not taken up in Committee of the Whole,
and Mr. Clay had therefore no opportunity to
speak upon the subject, when it was first presented to the House.

But while these resolutions were debated in the
House of Representatives, the Senate had been
more practically prompt. They had already
passed bills for largely increasing the regular
army, even beyond what the administration

desired. When the Senate bill, for the increase of the army, came to the House and was taken up in Committee of the Whole, Mr. Clay improved the opportunity, not before accorded him, to speak upon the subject. He commenced his remarks by stating that he should not complain of the course of proceeding which had been adopted, except for its effect in preventing him from participating in the debate, and assuming his share in the responsibility for the measures which the exigency of the times, in his opinion, demanded.

Mr. Clay urged the raising of a large army, and reasoned that upon the mere consideration of economy, a large and effective force was the best. "I do not stand," he said, "on this floor as the advocate of standing armies in the time of peace; but when war becomes essential, I *am* the advocate of raising able and vigorous armies to insure its success." Against the danger of the domination of a standing army over the liberties of the people, he opposed their general political information, and the fact of the existence of a powerful militia, "ready to point their bayonets to the breast of any tyrant who may attempt to crush their freedom." And in reply to those who

feared the danger of invasion, Mr. Clay said:
"Paris was taken, and all France consequently
subjugated. London might be subdued, and
England would fall before the conqueror. But
the population and strength of this country are
concentrated in no one place. Philadelphia may
be invaded — New York or Boston may fall —
every sea-port may be taken, but the country will
remain free. The whole of our territory this side
of the Alleghanies may be invaded, still liberty
will not be subdued. * * * The national
government; one or more of the state sovereignties, may be annihilated—the country will yet be
safe."

Such was Mr. Clay's earnestness and ardor in
the war cause. His expressions seem to us, at
this distance of time, like hyperbole; and his
contempt for all the dangers of war, like extravagance. As we have before remarked, he was
the representative of the young men, who probably desired to emulate the course of their elders,
who were enjoying, in old age, the dignity won
by service in the days of the Revolution, and the
troublesome times which followed. These same
old men were not yet out of the national councils,
and their cautious policy, had it been followed,

would not have precipitated war, though they might have been driven to it at last, after even longer delay. They knew the dangers and difficulties of a state of warfare, and the high price at which whatever is won by war is purchased. "Young America" took the direction out of the hands of the old statesman; for even President Madison never heartily sympathised with the zeal of the younger and more enthusiastic members of the war party.

Mr. Clay himself, after the experience obtained during the war he had so zealously supported, spake in a tone which contrasts strongly with the sentiments which we have quoted above. In 1811, he argued that although nothing were left of the national government, still "the country would be safe." In 1818, he said "it is not every cause of war which should lead to war. War is one of those dreadful scourges that so shakes the foundations of society, overturns or changes the characters of governments, interrupts or destroys the pursuit of private happiness, brings, in short, misery and wretchedness in so many forms, and at last is in its issue so doubtful and hazardous, that nothing but dire necessity can justify an appeal to arms." Experience teaches—and that course is ever safest which, though impelled by the activity of youthful and ardent actors, like Mr. Clay in 1811, is guided and moderated by older men, whose monitor is memory of the past.

Much of the warmth and extravagance of public speeches are attributable to the excitement of debate. Under its influence, men say more than they intend; more than, under circumstances favorable to calm reflection, they could utter. The terror of the advocates of a war with Great Britain was, at this time, John Randolph of Roanoke. Mr. Randolph was not a member of the Federal party, for in that case his attacks would have been less feared. He claimed to belong to the democratic side of the House, and as the war was a democratic measure, his resistance had a double weight. Mr. Randolph's style of oratory — discursive yet pointed — sarcastic, severe, and full of caustic wit, made him the most dangerous opponent that party or individual could have to deal with. It is said that Mr. Clay owed his election as Speaker to the hope that his known fearlessness and dignity of character might hold Randolph in check.

Mr. Randolph had been, in 1811, eleven years in the House of Representatives. His first utterance there was characteristic. On account of his extremely youthful appearance, the Speaker said to him, as he presented himself to take the oath of office, "Are you old enough, sir, to be eligible?" "Ask my constituents," was the only answer that Randolph designed to make to this inquiry. Mr. Randolph's secession from the regular democratic ranks occurred during Jefferson's administration. He voted against a resolution which was introduced to cease importation from Great Britain. Through Madison's administration, he strenuously opposed the war measures, and all that tended to strengthen army or navy, or to give the nation a military character; and in opposition to the measures now directly before the House, Mr. Randolph had made one of his most effective speeches. To him, as well as others, Mr. Clay was replying; and as they had dwelt much upon the power, and extolled the national character of Great Britain, he took the opposite side with a natural, though excessive warmth.

The bill under discussion passed the House by a large majority—ninety-four to thirty-four. Next in order came provisions for a Navy, the account of which we reserve for another chapter.

CHAPTER IX.

THE NAVY UNDER JEFFERSON — TIMID PROJECT OF MR. MADISON'S CABINET — REMONSTRANCES OF NAVAL OFFI-CERS — BILL TO INCREASE THE NAVY — SPEECH OF MR. CLAY—NAVAL HISTORY OF THE WAR OF 1812.

THE policy of Mr. Jefferson had been decidedly against a navy. When he came into office, in 1801, he found a law enacted by the Congress which expired as his term commenced, which law was designed to put the Navy on a peace establishment. This act empowered the President to sell any or all of the vessels of the Navy, with the exception of thirteen of the frigates. But the design of the law was not to extinguish or prevent the increase of the navy. By the same act, $500,000 (half a million) annually, were appropriated, toward the completion of six seventy-four-gun ships, authorised in 1798.

Under Mr. Jefferson's administration, all the vessels in the navy, except the thirteen frigates, and one small cruiser of twelve guns, were sold.

The appropriation for the seventy-fours was discontinued, and the timber collected for them was cut up to build gun-boats. The loss from the navy of the vessels sold was not much to be regretted, as they were mostly of imperfect frames, or poor models; but they should certainly have been replaced by something better than gun-boats. The whole number sold was twenty, carrying from twelve to twenty-four guns each, and nine galleys.

From 1801 to 1811, not a frigate was added to the navy. Of the thirteen in existence in 1801, one—the Philadelphia—had been destroyed, and three had fallen into decay, leaving nine only. One hundred and seventy gun-boats had been built, and nine small vessels added, carrying from twelve to eighteen guns. The impression was prevalent, that it was impossible to keep a navy at sea in the face of the overwhelming force of Great Britain, which embraced not less than a thousand sail. A project was actually entertained by the President to lay up in ordinary the few vessels which the United States possessed, to keep them from falling into the hands of the enemy! This policy had been determined on, but was changed by the efforts of two officers of the navy.

Captains Bainbridge and Stewart, happening to be at the seat of government, were shown copies of orders to Commodore Rodgers, not to leave New York, but to keep the vessels under his command in port, to form part of its harbor defence. They obtained an audience of President Madison, and convinced him of the impolicy and of the ruinous effect of such a course. Still the Cabinet, the President's constitutional advisers, adhered to their opinion. The two naval officers then addressed a letter to the President, who, after reading their arguments, took upon himself to change the plan. It is said that some members of the Cabinet consoled themselves with the reflection that if the vessels ventured out they would soon be taken; the administration would be saved the expense and trouble of maintaining them, and thus be enabled to devote all its care to the army.* So little do nations, as well as individuals, understand their true strength!

A bill was reported in the House of Representatives, in the spring of 1812, providing for ten new frigates, and a dock for repairs. The members of the Naval Committee, by whom the bill was reported, hinted in their speeches at a

* Cooper's Naval History.

much larger force than this. But there was a very determined opposition to the support of a navy; a subject upon which, as we have seen, even the President and his Cabinet hesitated. Henry Clay raised his strong voice in defence of the naval arm. We make some extracts from his speech:

"It appeared to Mr. Clay a little extraordinary that so much, as it seemed to him unreasonable jealousy should exist against the naval establishment. If," said he, "we look back to the period of the formation of the Constitution, it will be found that no such jealousy was then excited. In placing the physical force of the nation at the disposal of Congress, the convention manifested much greater apprehension of abuse in the power given to raise armies than in that to provide a navy. In reference to the navy, Congress is put under no restrictions; but with respect to the army — that description of force which has been so often employed to subvert the liberties of mankind — they are subjected to limitations designed to prevent the abuse of this dangerous power. But it was not his intention to detain the Committee, by a discussion on the comparative utility and safety of these two kinds of force.

He would, however, be indulged in saying, that he thought gentlemen had wholly failed in maintaining the position they had assumed, that the fall of maritime powers was attributable to their navies. They have told you that Carthage, Genoa, and Venice, and other nations, had navies, and notwithstanding were finally destroyed. But have they shown, by a train of argument, that their overthrow was in any degree attributable to their maritime greatness? Have they attempted, even, to show that there exists, in the nature of this power, a necessary tendency to destroy the nation using it? Assertion is substituted for argument; inferences not authorised by historical facts are arbitrarily drawn; things unconnected with each other are associated together;—a very logical mode of reasoning, it must be admitted! In the same way, he could demonstrate how idle and absurd our attachments are to freedom itself. He might say, for instance, that Greece and Rome had forms of free government, and that they no longer exist; and, deducing their fall from their devotion to liberty, the conclusion in favor of despotism would very satisfactorily follow! He demanded what there is in the nature and construction of maritime power, to excite the fears that have been indulged? Do gentlemen really apprehend, that a body of seamen will abandon their proper element, and placing themselves under an aspiring chief, will erect a throne to his ambition? Will they deign to listen to the voice of history, and learn how chimerical are these apprehensions?" Mr. Clay did not conceive it practicable to create a fleet which could cope with Great Britain; but he did think it within the power of the nation to provide a naval force adequate to protect our harbors, coasting trade, and inland navigation. He argued the necessity of a maritime power, from the necessity of commerce to a nation's greatness. "But," he said, "from the arguments of gentlemen, it would seem to be questioned if foreign commerce is worth the kind of protection insisted upon. What is this foreign commerce which has become suddenly so inconsiderable? It has, with very trifling aid from other sources, defrayed the expenses of government ever since the adoption of the present constitution; maintained an expensive and successful war with the Indians; a war with the Barbary powers; a quasi war with France; sustained the charges of suppressing two insurrections, and extinguished upwards of forty-six millions of the public debt. In revenue, it has, since the year 1789, yielded one hundred and ninety-one millions of dollars. During the first four years after the commencement of the present government, the revenue averaged only about two millions annually, or became equivalent to a capital of two hundred and fifty millions of dollars, at an interest of six per centum per annum. And if our commerce be re-established, it will, in the course of time, net a sum for which we are scarcely furnished with figures in arithmetic. Taking the average of the last nine years (comprehending, of course, the season of the embargo,) our exports average upward of thirty-seven millions of dollars, which is equivalent to a capital of more than six hundred millions of dollars at six per centum interest; all of which must be lost in the event of a destruction of foreign commerce. In the abandonment of that commerce is also involved the sacrifice of our brave tars, who have engaged in the pursuit from which they derive subsistence and support, under the confidence that government would afford them that just protection which is due to all. They will be driven into foreign employment, for

9*

it is vain to expect that they will renounce their habits of life."

As a verification of Mr. Clay's predictions, we may remark that the exports of the country, embracing domestic products only, now exceed one hundred millions annually; and if we include the foreign articles re-shipped, the amount will be increased some twenty-five millions more. The valuable coasting and internal trade of the United States, especially since the acquisition of California, is another vast source of business and employment for our mariners and others connected with the shipping and transportation interests. The number of vessels built annually is nearly two thousand, about one-fifth of which are steam-boats, and another fifth vessels of the larger classes. This annual supply is more than the whole loss during the war of 1812, by capture or otherwise. The character of the American mercantile marine is now second to none in the world. Vessels under the American flag successfully compete with British ships in her own carrying trade between the mother country and her distant possessions. The flag of the United States is seen upon every sea, and is everywhere respected. Mr. Clay mentioned as a remarkable fact, in the speech above quoted, that an American vessel had arrived at Leghorn from Pittsburgh. It is frequently the case now that ships depart from cities still farther inland upon our great rivers; but it is proper to remark that they do not return to the place of their first clearance. They can descend these rivers, but not ascend them; and the purpose of economy is served, in the first instance, by launching them where the timber for their frames can be most easily procured.

The number of vessels in the United States' Navy now, is still less than one hundred, including ten seventy-four-gun ships, and twenty-five frigates. The steam arm of the service, which has come into use since the war with Great Britain, is now rapidly increasing. The annual expense of the naval service averages about seven millions, including the mail service between this country and Great Britain.

During the war of 1812, the gallant little navy of the United States won a distinction which placed our country among the chief naval powers, and demonstrated that the nautical skill of the British seamen has not deteriorated by being transferred to a new country. "Brother Jou' than" has proved worthy of his parentage. We have not space, nor would it be in keeping with our purpose, to enter into war details, by land or sea. Suffice it to say, that the captures by the United States' Navy and privateers amounted, during the war, to seventeen hundred and fifty, leaving out of the count the vessels which were re-captured. The British Navy captured of American vessels, including gun-boats, sixteen hundred and eighty-three. The United States came out of the war with a naval reputation which they have never lost. Since that date, the services rendered to commerce and science by explorations and surveys, have more than justified the friends of the navy in their defence of its establishment and support.

We need hardly state that the bill which Mr. Clay advocated was passed, and proved the commencement of a more liberal policy toward the navy than had hitherto prevailed in the party with which he acted. The small appropriation ($500,000 in all) which the bill provided, was followed by more and larger grants. Experience has shown that the young statesman's predictions relative to the importance and value of commerce to the nation, were rather within than beyond the truth.

CHAPTER X.

HENRY'S EMBASSY — DECLARATION OF WAR.

THERE were some indications of an intention in the Cabinet to take a step which would have given Henry Clay a place among the military heroes of his country. It is a historical fact that the moderation, prudence, or hesitancy of Mr. Madison's character, delayed positive action until urged by the Congressional war-party, and of this the soul was Henry Clay. Forty years have produced such a change in the public sentiment in relation to war and its evils, that it is hard to try the friends of the war of 1812 by our present standard of opinion. Yet we have seen, in a recent case, war produced on much less pressing occasion than that of 1812 — if indeed there was any pressing occasion for the late war with Mexico. There was everything to irritate the popular mind against Great Britain; and not the least grievance was the despatching an emissary into New England, to labor to produce disunion, or neutrality. It is true that this agent does not seem to have reached the ear of any responsible party, or to have produced any impression; and his haunts while in Boston exhibited him as a person of moral associations as low as his political employment was disgraceful. And it is true also that the British Government subsequently disavowed having given authority for his proceedings, though his employment by a colonial governor was certainly a fact. The truth respecting him appears to be, that he was a man with a natural proclivity for dirty work; and that he suggested and procured the employment, which resulted in nothing but furnishing new cause of exasperation to the American people. He concluded by selling his correspondence with the colonial authorities and the British Ministry, to the American Government.

This correspondence was transmitted to Congress. There was nothing incredible in the statement that Great Britain was prepared to take advantage of any difficulty among the states preparing for war against her, or to create, if possible, a difficulty where none existed. It would be a part of that diplomatic strategy which nations striving to injure each other, or to defend themselves, often practise.

The next prominent event in order of time, is the second embargo, as it was termed, the first having occurred during Jefferson's administration. Mr. Randolph and others strenuously opposed — Mr. Clay earnestly defended it, and predicted that war would take place in sixty days. In enumerating the causes of offence which Great Britain had furnished, Mr. Clay referred to the mission of Henry as that of "an emissary, sent to one of our principal cities to excite civil war." The Embargo Act, prepared by the Committee on Foreign Relations before the President's Message was received, and reported almost simultaneously, was carried through the House, seventy to forty-one, in secret session on the same day. It passed the Senate on the next day, with an amendment lengthening the time of the embargo from sixty to ninety days, which amendment was concurred in. The bill — declared emphatically by its framers to be a war measure — thus became a law.

On the 1st of June, 1812, the President transmitted confidentially to Congress a Message, in which he recapitulated the oppressive, unfriendly,

and unjust proceedings of Great Britain, and
presented the two nations as in a peculiar attitude — war against the United States, so far as
Great Britain was concerned, and peace toward
Great Britain, so far as the United States was
considered; and he submitted the choice of further endurance, or of warlike resistance, to Congress, as "a solemn question which the Constitution wisely confides to the legislative department
of the government."

The Message was referred to the Committee on
Foreign Relations, and in two days thereafter,
John C. Calhoun, the chairman, reported a bill
declaring war against Great Britain. It was
passed, seventy-nine to forty-nine. No speeches
are recorded, and the only efforts made by the
opposition, were by ineffectual motions intended
to defeat or delay, which were at once voted
down. Though so summarily passed by the
House, the Senate held the bill two weeks with
closed doors. On the 18th of June, it was returned to the House with an amendment author-
ising the issue of commissions to privateers. On
the same day, the amendment was concurred in
by the House, the bill was passed, and received
the President's approval; and on the next day

was issued the President's Proclamation in pursuance of the Act.

Thus in sixty days—with a few days' grace for Senatorial delays—was Mr. Clay's prediction verified, and the country was at war with Great Britain. The simultaneous preparation of the Embargo Act and Message of the President—both done out of the House, the latter of course—and the wonderful celerity with which the House acted on the War Message, argue a closer connection between the Executive and his friends in Congress, than more modern usage permits. But the history of the times shows that several members of the House, at the head of whom was Henry Clay, had nearly as much voice in the President's councils, as his Cabinet proper. Presidential messages followed Congressional conclaves with the Executive; and the message recommending or suggesting war, was preceded by a conference with Mr. Clay and others, the subject of which was, at the time, no secret. There is no doubt that Mr. Clay was as active in procuring war measures, as he was energetic in defending them, and patriotic in his efforts to maintain the cause of his country. His zealous eloquence, in

10

Kentucky, added to the zeal and fire of the citizens of that warlike State.

It is related of Demosthenes, that courageous as he was in his orations against the enemies of Athens, in the field his valor failed him, and he fled. We cannot suppose that Henry Clay would have resembled the Athenian in this particular, though no modern orator has more nearly approached the father of eloquence in power of persuasion, and command of the minds and actions of others. Mr. Madison proposed, as hinted at the commencement of this chapter, to nominate Mr. Clay to the Senate a Major-General, when making the new appointments upon the increase of the army. We can now only speculate on the probabilities of Mr. Clay's fitness or unfitness; but so far as patriotism and courage go to make up the qualifications of a military officer, there can be little doubt of his fitness. His laurels have, however, been won in a more peaceful field; and the services he has rendered to his country are of a nature for which experience has proved him eminently fitted; for his best fame rests on his course since the war.

As we have already said, he was the soul of the war-party, his ardent and impetuous character communicating zeal and hope, when a more cautious man would have failed. It was a fearful crisis in the history of our country, when the fire of youth prevailed over the caution of age, and a nation lamentably deficient in means and in preparation, was thrust into a contest with the most powerful nation on the globe. If ever wars are necessary, the strongest plea existed for this war; and if any man, more than another, merits the reputation of procuring its declaration, that credit is due to Henry Clay.

His most effective and eloquent war-speech was on the question of increasing the army, in the session of 1812–13. We cannot make extracts without the quotation of passages perpetuating old subjects of bitterness, and reviving charges against American statesmen and parties; — charges then received in the heat of party acrimony, but now forgotten. We therefore here close the narrative of Mr. Clay's connection, as a legislator, with the war of 1812. .

CHAPTER XI.

MR. CLAY APPOINTED PEACE COMMISSIONER — RETORT
COURTEOUS—BRITISH DEMANDS—LONG NEGOTIATION—
THE TREATY — REJOICINGS AND COMPLAINTS — THE
LONDON TIMES — MR. CLAY'S SPEECH IN LEXINGTON —
ANECDOTE.

IN the year 1813, the good offices of Russia
were tendered as mediator between the United
States and Great Britain. The President appointed Gallatin and Bayard to act jointly with
J. Q. Adams, the American Minister at St.
Petersburgh, in conducting this negotiation; and
those gentlemen sailed for Europe in a private
vessel, protected by a "cartel," or letter of protection from the British admiral. But the
British Government declined the mediation of
Russia, and offered to treat directly with the
American Commissioners in London; or, if that
were not agreeable, in Gottenburgh. The President appointed Adams, Bayard, Henry Clay, and
Jonathan Russel, the Commissioners under this

proposition, and afterwards added Gallatin to the number, making five; and the place of meeting was changed from Gottenburgh to Ghent.

Mr. Clay took leave of the House January 19th, 1814, resigning his seat, and receiving a vote of thanks nearly unanimous; nine only voting in the negative, out of 123 votes cast. Having presided in such difficult times, when party feeling ran so very high, so general an expression of good will is a highly honorable testimony to the impartiality of Mr. Clay. Messrs. Clay and Russel sailed in February, in the U. S. ship John Adams, carrying the protection of a cartel. The American Commissioners in due time assembled at Ghent, but the British Commissioners did not meet them there until August. The treaty was not signed until the 24th of December, 1814. Much time was spent in negotiation, and much firmness was necessary to resist the enormous demands of the British Commissioners. Flushed with their victory over Napoleon, they came into the negotiation prepared to dictate terms, as to a conquered people.

There is an anecdote of Mr. Clay which belongs in this connection, and is too good to be lost. Mr. Goulburn, one of the British Commis-

10*

sioners, forwarded to Mr. Clay, at Brussels, a London paper containing the official account of the burning of the public buildings at Washington, by the British forces. Mr. Goulburn made an apology for the disagreeable nature of the intelligence, but presumed that Mr. Clay would probably still desire to hear the latest intelligence from America. It so happened that the French journals were just re-publishing the account of the British defeat on Lake Champlain. Mr. Clay returned Mr. Goulburn's civility by enclosing to him a French paper with that intelligence, accompanied by a similar apology.

Of the spirit in which the more violent British prints discussed the question of a treaty, something may be judged from the following paragraphs: "It was strongly reported on 'Change, that it is the fixed determination of our government [the British] not to suffer the Americans to fish upon the Banks of Newfoundland, and that no American vessel will be permitted to pass the Cape of Good Hope; so that the whole of the China trade will be taken from them." The London Times of May 20, 1814, had the following:

"Bonaparte is fallen — Madison is disgraced

and discomfited, and Great Britain has the means of inflicting ample and deserved vengeance. Lo! the pupils of liberality, the philanthropists, the sworn advocates of foreign perfidy and treachery, step forth and deprecate the very idea of justice, or of prudent precaution against future insult. But they will no more be listened to now, than when they so urgently pleaded the cause of the monster, Bonaparte. It is true that negotiators of great respectability have been appointed on the part of Great Britain, to meet the Genevese democrat Gallatin, the furious orator Clay, the surly Bayard, and Mr. Russel, the worthy defender of the forged revocation of the Berlin and Milan decree.

"We have, however, good reason to believe that the British diplomatists will not condescend to discuss the impudent nonsense called the American doctrine, about impressment and native allegiance, which was in truth a mere pretext for war on the part of Mr. Madison; but they will enter into the true merits of the question — the unprovoked and unprincipled attack on Canada; they will demand full security against a renewal of this atrocious outrage; they will insist on the safe and undivided possession of the lakes; the abandonment of the Newfoundland fishery; and the restitution of Louisiana and the usurped territory in Florida."

Such were the newspaper notions of what the British Commissioners should demand; and the claims with which those gentlemen entered upon the negotiation, were little short of what the Times demanded. The Commissioners claimed that the United States should set off a permanent Indian territory for the British Indian allies, between the United States and Canada; that we should dismantle our forts, and withdraw our vessels on the great lakes; and that Great Britain should keep possession of a portion of Maine which she had seized, east of the river Penobscot.

The treaty, as signed, contained no concessions to Great Britain; and, as in all treaties where nations are desirous of peace, no grants were finally insisted on by either side. If Great Britain did not, in terms, relinquish her political claim, "once a subject always a subject," neither did the United States admit it; and the effect of the war has practically been to abolish impressment of men on board of American vessels. The British lost the right of navigating the Mississippi. The Americans lost that of curing fish on

the shores of the Gulf of St. Lawrence. The
fisheries have since been arranged by a separate
treaty, under which United States vessels may
catch fish, except within three miles (a cannon-
shot) of the shore; but they cannot land them,
as formerly, for the purpose of dressing and
curing. It was proposed, in the discussion, to
place these privileges as they were before the
war; but Mr. Clay refused his assent, and the
result proves his sagacity. The boundaries
between the two powers, on this continent, have
since been determined both in Maine, and west
of the great lakes.

The *people* of both countries were delighted at
the proclamation of peace. Great rejoicings took
place in this country, and in the other. A sketch
of the terms on which the treaty had been concluded, was read to the audiences in the London
theatres. In the provincial towns, there were
great rejoicings; particularly in those which had
most intercourse with the United States. In our
own country, the opponents of the war insisted
that nothing had been gained, though the wiser
were satisfied with any peace rather than war.
But if there were those who insisted that the
Americans had gained nothing, there were others

in Great Britain who claimed no honor to British arms or negotiation. The London Times of the 30th December, 1815, not having yet heard of the Battle of New Orleans, said :

"We have attempted to force our principles on America, *and have failed*. We have retired from the combat with the stripes yet bleeding on our backs—with the various recent defeats at Plattsburgh, and on Lake Champlain, unavenged. To make peace at such a moment, it will be said, betrays a deadness to the feelings of honor, and shows a timidity of disposition inviting further insult. If we could have pointed to America overthrown, we should surely have stood on much higher ground at Vienna, and everywhere else, than we possibly can do now. Even yet, however, if we could but close the war with some great naval triumph, the reputation of our maritime greatness might be partially restored; but to say that it has not hitherto suffered in the estimation of all Europe, and what is worse, of America herself, is to belie common sense and universal experience. 'Two or three of our ships have struck to a force vastly superior.' No, not two or three, but many on the ocean, and whole squadrons on the lakes; and the numbers are to

be viewed with relation to the comparative mag-
nitude of the two navies. Scarcely is there an
American ship of war which has not to boast a
victory over the British flag; scarcely a British
ship in thirty or forty that has beaten an American."

The mortified editor of the Times had still to
hear of the Battle of New Orleans, after the
above was penned. The naval engagements
which took place after the signing of the treaty,
added to the list of American successes. The
treaty took effect on land as soon as ratified; and
on the ocean at certain specified times, to allow
opportunity to hear of the proclamation of peace.
There were three United States vessels at sea
when peace was proclaimed — the Constitution,
the Hornet, and the Peacock. The Constitution
captured the Cyane and Levant, engaging both at
once; but afterward lost the Levant in a squadron
of British vessels. The Hornet captured the
Penguin, but it became necessary to destroy her
prize; and the Peacock captured the Nautilus,
but restored her on the day following.

Mr. Clay returned to the United States almost
with the honors of a conqueror. At no time was
he more highly popular than at the close of the

war; for up to this date, the acts of his life
which partisan opposition has effectively opposed
to him, had not occurred. As we have presented
him to our readers as the most active supporter
of the war of 1812, we give, in justice to him,
his views of its consequences. At a dinner in
Lexington, Mr. Clay replied to a complimentary
sentiment in a speech, from which the following
is an extract :—

"I feel myself called upon, by the sentiment
just expressed, to return my thanks in behalf of
my colleagues and myself. I do not, and I am
quite sure they do not feel, that in the service
alluded to they are at all entitled to the compliment which has been paid to them. We could
not do otherwise than reject the demand made by
the other party; and if our labors finally terminated in an honorable peace, it was owing to
causes on this side of the Atlantic, and not to
any exertion of ours. Whatever diversity of
opinion may have existed as to the declaration of
the war, there are some points on which all may
look back with proud satisfaction. The first
relates to the time of the conclusion of the peace.
Had it been made immediately after the treaty
of Paris, we should have retired humiliated from

the contest, believing that we had escaped from the severe chastisement with which we were threatened, and that we owed to the generosity and magnanimity of the enemy, what we were incapable of commanding by our arms. That magnanimity would have been the theme of every tongue, and of every press, abroad and at home. We should have retired, unconscious of our own strength, and unconscious of the utter inability of the enemy, with his whole undivided force, to make any serious impression upon us. Our military character, then in the lowest state of degradation, would have been unretrieved. Fortunately for us, Great Britain chose to try the issue of the last campaign. And that has demonstrated, in the repulse before Baltimore; the retreat from Plattsburgh; the hard-fought action on the Niagara frontier; and in that most glorious day, the eighth of January, that we have always possessed the finest elements of military composition; and that a proper use of them only, was necessary to insure for the army and militia a fame as imperishable as that which the navy had previously acquired.

"Another point, which appears to me to afford the highest consolation, is that we fought the

11

most powerful nation, perhaps, in existence, single-handed and alone, without any sort of alliance. More than thirty years had Great Britain been maturing her physical means, which she had rendered as efficacious as possible, by skill, by discipline, and by actual service. Proudly boasting of the conquest of Europe, she vainly flattered herself with the easy conquest of America also. Her veterans were put to flight or defeated, while all Europe — I mean the governments of Europe — was gazing with cold indifference, or sentiments of positive hatred of us, upon the arduous contest. Hereafter no monarch can assert claims of gratitude upon us, for assistance rendered in the hour of danger.

"There is another view of which the subject of the war is fairly susceptible. From the moment that Great Britain came forward at Ghent with her extravagant demands, the war totally changed in character. It became, as it were, a new war. It was no longer an American war, prosecuted for redress of British aggressions upon American rights, but became a British war, prosecuted for objects of British ambition, to be accompanied by American sacrifices. And what were those demands? They consisted of the erection of a barrier between Canada and the United States, to be formed by cutting off from Ohio, and some of the Territories, a country more extensive than Great Britain; containing thousands of freemen, who were to be abandoned to their fate, and creating a new power totally unknown upon the continent of America; of the disarming of our fortresses and naval power on the lakes, with the surrender of the military occupation of those waters to the enemy; and of an arrondissement for two British provinces. These demands, boldly asserted, and one of them declared to be a *sine qua non*, were finally relinquished. Taking this view of the subject, if there be loss of reputation by either party in the terms of peace, who has sustained it?

"The effects of the war are highly satisfactory. Abroad, our character, which at the time of its declaration was in the lowest state of degradation, is raised to the highest point of elevation. It is impossible for any American to visit Europe without being sensible of this agreeable change, in the personal attentions which he receives, in the praises which are bestowed upon our past exertions, and the predictions which are made as to our future prospects. At home, a government which, at its formation, was apprehended by its best friends, and predicted by its enemies, to be incapable of standing the shock, is found to answer all the purposes of its institution. In spite of the errors which have been committed, (and errors undoubtedly have been committed,) aided by the spirit and patriotism of the people, it is demonstrated to be as competent to the objects of effective war, as it has been before proved to be to the concerns of a season of peace. Government has thus acquired strength and confidence. Our prospects for the future are of the brightest kind. With every reason to count on the permanence of peace, it remains only for the government to determine upon military and naval establishments adapted to the growth and extension of our country, and its rising importance, keeping in view a gradual, but not burdensome, increase of the navy; to provide for the payment of the interest, and the redemption of the public debt, and for the current expenses of the government. For all these objects, the existing sources of the revenue promise not only to be abundantly sufficient, but will probably leave ample scope to the exercise of the judgment of Congress, in selecting for repeal, modification, or abolition, those which may be found most oppressive, inconvenient, or unproductive."

Respecting the phrase *sine qua non*, an amusing anecdote was related by Mr. Clay; for he had a pleasant custom of enlivening a dry subject by an amusing story. "While the Commissioners were still abroad," said Mr. Clay, "there appeared a report of the negotiations, or letters relative thereto. Several quotations from my remarks, or letters touching certain stipulations in the treaty, reached Kentucky, and were read by my constituents. Among them was an eccentric fellow who went by the nickname of 'Old Sandusky,' and he was reading one of these letters, one evening, to a small collection of his neighbors. As he read on, he came to the sentence, 'This must be deemed a *sine qua non*.'

"'What's a *sine qua non*?' asked half a dozen voices.

"Old Sandusky was a little perplexed, but his native shrewdness was as good as Latin. '*Sine qua non*?' said the old fellow, slowly repeating the question; 'why *sine qua non* is three islands in Passamaquoddy Bay, and Harry Clay is the last man to give them up! No *sine qua non*, he says, no treaty, and he'll stick to it!'"

CHAPTER XII.

MR. CLAY'S ELOQUENCE — FRANKFORT AND THE HAT —
MADAME DE STAEL AND WELLINGTON — BONAPARTE —
MR. CLAY'S ADVICE TO YOUNG MEN.

MR. CLAY was now (1815) in the zenith of his popularity, and the pride of his manhood. The epithet "furious orator," which the British press applied to him, referred only to his energetic and zealous efforts against what he deemed abuses, or in denunciation of what he considered unpatriotic or dangerous measures — declamations against foes abroad, or errors at home. He could be pathetic, or he could be playful. The following description of his manner, gesture, and appearance, is from an anonymous writer, but strikes us forcibly with its graphic distinctness. "Every muscle of the orator's face was at work. His whole body seemed agitated, as if each part was instinct with a separate life; and his small white hand, with its blue veins apparently distended almost to bursting, moved gracefully, but with all the energy of rapid and vehement gesture. The appearance of the speaker seemed that of a pure intellect, wrought to its mightiest energies, and brightly shining through the thin and transparent veil of flesh that invested it."

The possession of a talent for repartee and sarcasm, and the ability to say amusing things at the expense of others, however effective in carrying a point, are not always safe for the speaker. During the rejoicings which followed the proclamation of peace, Mr. Clay had an opportunity to recall a humorous affront which he had once given to the lieges of Frankfort. At a public dinner, he paid the capital some very handsome compliments, alluding to a diverting passage in his legislative experience many years before. The project of removing the seat of government was before the House; Mr. Clay argued in favor of the removal. Frankfort is walled in on all sides by precipitous hills — romantic and pictu resque — with the beautiful Kentucky River cutting its way through these natural barriers Nevertheless, Frankfort does seem, if we choose to employ a grotesque comparison, like a great pit.

'The place presents," said Mr. Clay, "the model of an inverted hat. Frankfort is the body of the hat, and the lands adjacent are the brim. To change the figure, it is nature's great penitentiary. Who that gets in, can get out? And if you would know the bodily condition of the prisoners, look at those persons in the gallery!" As Mr. Clay said this, he gave a sweep with his hand, which directed the attention of the legislature to some half dozen persons who happened to be lounging there, and who, finding the attention of the House was directed to them, disappeared with the utmost precipitation behind post, pillar, railing, or whatever could offer a friendly covert. The House burst into a laugh at the ludicrousness of the incident, and voted to abdicate the penitentiary. But the measure did not finally pass, for Frankfort is still the capital of Kentucky.

Since we are repeating anecdotes, we may relate one or two more which are connected with Mr. Clay's mission to Europe. While in Paris, after the signing of the treaty of Ghent, Madame de Stael pleasantly told him that the Americans were her debtors, inasmuch as she had been doing battle for them in London, during the war. This was magnanimous in the lady; for she thus furnished one example, at least, of a defender or apologist of the war, with no Bonapartean prejudices; for Madame de Stael, until the downfall of Napoleon, was an exile from France. Napoleon exceedingly disliked her. Mr. Clay replied, that "the Americans had heard of her good offices, and were not ungrateful for them." This was not necessarily a mere compliment; for no woman in modern times has possessed more influence, by her pen and her conversation, than Madame de Stael.

During the same conversation, Madame de Stael remarked to Mr. Clay, that the British Government had proposed, during the war, to send out the Duke of Wellington to command the British forces in America. "I am very sorry," replied Mr. Clay, "that they did not send his Grace."

"And why, sir?" inquired the lady.

"Because, madam, if he had beaten us, we should only have been in the condition of all Europe, without disgrace; but if we had been so fortunate as to beat the Duke, it would have added greatly to the renown of our arms."

A few days afterward, when the Duke and Mr. Clay met at her house, Madame de Stael, with

9

playful malice, repeated the conversation. The Duke answered, "Had I been sent on such an errand, and been so successful as to conquer the Americans, it would have been regarded as one of my proudest triumphs." It is one of the absurdities of war that men can thus make badinage of it — that, enemies to-day, to morrow they can be on terms of complimentary intercourse; or, in other words, that those who have really no feeling but complaisance and courtesy, can be placed, by a proclamation, in a position to aim at each other's destruction!

So wonderful, too, are the reverses of war! In a preceding chapter, we have speculated on the chance which once existed, that Napoleon might be the founder of a military colony in North America — perhaps a military despot on this continent. This was averted by the demonstrations of Great Britain against him, and the sale of Louisiana to the United States. It was thought that the mighty conqueror, shorn of his power at Waterloo, might come to this country as a fugitive. It was suggested at the table of Lord Liverpool, in London, where Mr. Clay was one day a guest, that he might perhaps flee to the New World as an asylum.

"Will he not give you some trouble, if he goes there?" asked Lord Liverpool.

"Not the least, my lord," replied Mr. Clay; "we shall be very glad to see him, will entertain him with all due rites of hospitality, and soon make him a good democrat." But Mr. Clay lived to see that foreign discomfited captains make very poor democrats. They are more apt to continue adventurers, and cannot settle down into the dull quiet of freedom without war.

Mr. Clay, on his return to America, found himself already re-elected to the House of Representatives. But as there were some doubts of the legality of an election while he was absent, a new canvass was ordered; and thus, twice elected, he was ready to resume his place. As before, he was chosen Speaker by a large vote; for it seemed that none but he could answer the exigencies of the post, in the minds of his contemporaries. The secret of influence so paramount over the minds of others, we may gather from his own declaration. No doubt natural fitness is all essential; but not even Henry Clay could become an apt debater without industry. In an address delivered by Mr. Clay to the students of a law school at Ballston, New York, a few years since, he said :

"I owe my success in life to one single fact, viz.: that at the age of twenty-seven I commenced, and continued for years, the process of daily reading and speaking upon the contents of some historical or scientific book. These off-hand efforts were made sometimes in a corn-field, at others in the forest, and not unfrequently in some distant barn, with the horse and the ox for my auditors. It is to this early practice of the great art of all arts, that I am indebted for the primary and leading impulses that stimulated me forward, and have shaped and moulded my entire subsequent destiny. Improve then, young gentlemen, the superior advantages you here enjoy. Let not a day pass without exercising your powers of speech. There is no power like that of oratory. Cæsar controlled men by exciting their fears; Cicero by captivating their affections and swaying their passions. The influence of the one perished with its author; that of the other continues to this day."

CHAPTER XIII.

ONE of the most reprehensible acts committed during the war of 1812, was the destruction of the public buildings and several private residences, in Washington, by a British force under General Ross. We have not space to go into particulars, and need only say that the defence of the capital—or rather neglect of defence—was as little creditable to American arms on the one side, as the destruction of the public buildings was to British magnanimity on the other.

The only public building spared was that which was used for the Patent Office and Post Office, which were under the same roof. A portion of this building was fitted up for the purposes of Congress, and during the one session that the national legislature met there, the project of changing the seat of government was introduced, but not carried. In the following year, 1815,

12

some of the citizens of Washington, moved, perhaps, by apprehension lest the question of change
should again be called up, erected a temporary
building, of which the government took a lease.
It is mentioned in contemporary prints, that the
lot on which this temporary capitol stood was, on
the fourth of July previous to the meeting of
Congress, a garden. The bricks of which it was
built were in the clay, and the timber still standing in the forests at that date.

One of the leading measures of this session
was the charter of a new United States Bank.
This subject we have anticipated in a previous
chapter. The first thought of the national councils was to provide for the public debt, now
amounting to over a hundred millions in stocks,
beside some twenty more of treasury notes, and
a great amount of unadjusted claims. The subject of taxation of course was a prominent one,
and engaged much attention. The President, in
his Message, had recommended discriminating
duties in favor of American industry. "In
adjusting the duties on imports to the objects of
revenue, the influence of the tariff on manufactures will necessarily present itself for consideration. * * * In selecting the branches more

especially entitled to the public patronage, a preference is obviously claimed by such as will relieve the United States from dependence on foreign supplies — ever subject to casual failures — for articles necessary for the public defence, or connected with the primary wants of individuals. It will be an additional recommendation of particular manufactures, when the materials for them are extensively drawn from our agriculture, and consequently impart and insure to that great fund of national prosperity and independence, an encouragement which cannot fail to be rewarded."

As an illustration of party changes, we may remark that the Federalists, as a party, now opposed the protective system, while the great body of the Democrats defended it; John Randolph, and a few of his friends, being the exceptions. Calhoun and Clay labored side by side for the tariff—Calhoun, who, in his later life, opposed nullification to protection. But the Federalists were chiefly representatives of commercial interests, and the Southern men represented cotton-growing states. American cotton, at that time, was repulsed in England by a duty; and the imported cotton goods which then came to America were chiefly of India cotton. American manufactures received an impetus during the war, which, taken in connection with the British duty discriminating in favor of India cotton, led the Southern men to suppose that their future market must be in America.

A tariff was enacted, but Mr. Clay was in favor of a much higher rate of duty than it imposed; arguing that, "the period of the termination of the war, during which the manufacturing industry of the country had received a powerful spring, was precisely that period when government was alike impelled, by duty and interest, to protect it against the admission of foreign fabrics, consequent upon a state of peace." Mr. Clay also argued the importance of preparation in peace for war; and laid down the principle that in time of peace we should look to foreign importations as the chief source of revenue, and in time of war to internal taxes. He referred to the still unsettled state of our relations with Spain, growing out of the Florida difficulty, which remained unadjusted, though the land in dispute was in part incorporated with Louisiana. He alluded to the congress of potentates then in session in Vienna. Their ideas of 'legitimate government' were carried to an extent destructive of every principle of liberty. We have seen these doctrines applied to create and overthrow dynasties at will. Do we know, he asked, whether we shall escape their influence?

The subject of the recognition of the Spanish-American republics was agitated in various forms, in Congress, from the period of which we write (1816) to the year 1822; when, upon the special recommendation of President Monroe, their independence was formally recognized by Congress. The matter had been embarrassed by the boundary dispute with Spain, as detailed in Chapter VI. of this volume; and the difference was not closed until, in 1821, the treaty with Spain in reference to Florida was ratified. By this treaty, all the Spanish claims east of the Mississippi were annulled, in consideration of the release of American claims against Spain. The boundary west of the Mississippi gave Texas, which had also been in dispute, to Spain.

The Tariff Bill, which passed at this session after a necessarily long debate, was based upon the principles propounded by the President. It classified the articles of import under three heads: Those of which a full domestic supply could be

12*

produced; those of which a partial supply can be manufactured; and those not produced at home at all, or in insufficient quantities. The last class of goods was taxed with a view to revenue solely. On the others, the rates were from twenty to twenty-five per cent. generally; but some specific duties were much higher. We shall have occasion, in a future chapter, to refer to the Tariff and the American system again; and for the present will confine ourselves to Mr. Clay's efforts in behalf of the sister republics on this continent. For to put the nation in an attitude to defend its position in regard to the American republics was, as we have already observed, one great reason with Mr. Clay for desiring a sufficient revenue.

Mr. Randolph was exceedingly severe upon the republics then struggling into existence, and as his remarks were made in a style characteristic of the man, we make a brief extract. There is a mixture of sound discernment and of extravagance in what he said — a strain of what would have been prophecy, if uttered in language a little less exaggerated. Our South American neighbors have not done so much credit to the name of republicans as we could have wished; and indeed, at this distance of time—nearly forty years—have hardly settled under their new institutions. Still, that they will become republics indeed, there remains now no room to doubt; and Mr. Clay's hopes for them will be realised.

"This struggle for liberty," Mr. Randolph said, "would turn out in the end something like the French liberty—a detestable despotism. You cannot make liberty out of Spanish matter—you might as well try to build a seventy-four out of pine saplings! What ideas had the Spaniards of rational liberty—of the trial by jury—of the right of habeas corpus—of the slow process by which this House moves and acts? None, sir, none! Expediency, necessity, the previous question, the inquisition—these were among the engines belonging to their ideas of government. The honorable Speaker [Mr. Clay] had told the House, on a recent occasion, that he saw instances of this or that in the British House of Commons; the honorable gentleman had been sent on a recent occasion to Europe—he had been near the field of Waterloo. He was afraid the honorable gentleman had caught the infection—that he had snuffed the carnage—and when a man once catches that infection, like that of ambition or avarice—whether taken by inoculation or in the natural way, the consequences are permanent. What, increase our standing army in a time of peace, on the suggestion that we are to go on a crusade in South America! Do I not understand the gentleman? [Mr. Clay here intimated a negative to this question.] I am sorry I did not," continued Mr. Randolph; "I labor under two great misfortunes: one is, that I can never understand the honorable Speaker; the other, that he can never understand me!"

In answer to charges like the foregoing against the Spanish patriots, Clay said: "It had been charged that the people of South America were incapable, from the ignorance and superstition which prevail among them, of achieving independence, or enjoying liberty. And to what cause was that ignorance and superstition owing? Was it not to the vices of their government? to the tyranny and oppression, hierarchal and political, under which they groaned? If Spain succeeded in riveting their chains upon them, would not that ignorance and superstition be perpetuated? For my part," said Mr. Clay, "I wish them independence. It is the first step toward improving their condition. Let them have free government if they are capable of enjoying it; but let them, at all events, have independence. I may be accused of an imprudent utterance of my feelings. I care not; for when the independence, the happiness, the liberty of a whole people is at stake, and that people our neighbors, our brethren, occupying a portion of the same continent, imitating our example, and participating in the same sympathies as ourselves, I will boldly avow my feelings and my wishes in their behalf, even at the risk of such an imputation."

Mr. Clay's speeches upon this subject are many in number, and we extract from them without regard to the order of time, such passages as did not depend for their interest upon contemporary circumstances, but are everywhere interesting, and at all times. The parallel in the following between the circumstances of the South American republics, and our own in its infancy, is well drawn : —

"Let us recollect the condition of the patriots: no minister here to spur on our government; no minister here to be rewarded by noble honors in consequence of the influence he is supposed to possess in our republic. No: their unfortunate case was what ours had been in 1778 and 1779;

their ministers, like our Franklins and Jays at that day, were skulking about Europe, imploring inexorable legitimacy for one kind look — some aid to terminate a war afflicting to humanity. Nay, their situation was worse than ours, for we had one great and magnanimous ally to recognise us; but no nation had stepped forward to acknowledge any of these provinces. Such disparity between the parties demanded a just attention to the interests of the party which was unrepresented. * * * We must pass condemnation upon the founders of our own liberty, and say that they were rebels, traitors, and that we are at this moment legislating without competent powers, before we can condemn South America. Our revolution was mainly directed against the mere theory of tyranny. We had suffered comparatively but little—we had in some respects been kindly treated; but our intrepid and intelligent fathers saw, in the usurpation of a power to levy an inconsiderable tax, the long train of oppressive acts which were to follow. They rose — they breasted the storm; they achieved our freedom. Spanish America for centuries has been doomed to the practical effects of an odious tyranny. If we were justified, she is more than justified.

"I am no propagandist. I would not seek to force upon other nations our principles and our liberty, if they do not want them. I would not disturb the repose even of a detestable despotism. But if an abused and oppressed people will their freedom; if they seek to establish it; if in truth they have established it; we have a right, as a sovereign power, to notice the fact, and to act as circumstances and our interest require. I will say, in the language of the venerated Father of my country, 'born in a land of liberty, my anxious recollections, my sympathetic feelings, and my best wishes are irresistibly excited, whensoever, in any country, I see an oppressed nation unfurl the banners of freedom.' Whenever I think of Spanish America, the image irresistibly forces itself upon my mind, of an elder brother whose education has been neglected, whose person has been abused and maltreated, and who has been disinherited by the unkindness of an unnatural parent. And when I contemplate the glorious struggle which that nation is now making, I think I behold that brother rising, by the power and energy of his fine native genius, to the manly rank which nature, and nature's God, intended for him.

"It is the doctrine of thrones that man is too ignorant to govern himself. Their partisans assert his incapacity in reference to all nations; if they cannot demand universal assent to the proposition, it is then demanded as to particular nations; and our pride and our presumption too often make converts of us. I contend that it is to arraign the dispositions of Providence himself, to suppose that he has created beings incapable of governing themselves, and to be trampled on by kings!

"But the House has been asked, and asked with a triumph worthy of a better cause, why recognise this republic? Where is the use of it? And is it possible that gentlemen can see no use in recognising this republic? For what did this republic [La Plata] fight? To be admitted into the family of nations. 'Tell the nations of the world,' says one of her statesmen, in his speech, 'that we already belong to their illustrious rank.' What would be the powerful consequences of a recognition of their claim? I ask my honorable friend before me [General Bloomfield] the highest sanction of whose judgment in favor of my pro-

BOLIVER READING CLAY'S SPEECH.

position I fondly anticipate, with what anxious solicitude, during our revolution, he and his glorious compatriots turned their eyes to Europe, and asked to be recognised? I ask him, the patriot of '76, how the heart rebounded with joy, on the information that France had recognised us? The moral influence of such a recognition on the patriot of South America, will be irresistible. He will derive assurance from it, of his not having fought in vain. In the constitution of our natures there is a point to which adversity may pursue us, without, perhaps, any worse effect than that of exciting new energy to meet it. Having reached that point, if no gleam of comfort breaks through the gloom, we sink beneath the pressure, yielding reluctantly to our fate, and in hopeless despair lose all stimulus to exertion. And is there not reason to fear such a fate for the patriots of La Plata?"

Such are a few specimens of the earnestness with which, year after year, Mr. Clay pleaded for the South American republics. His speeches were well known among those in whose cause they were uttered. The Spanish are an enthusiastic people, and admire chivalric and noble bearing; and the efforts of Henry Clay in their

13

behalf were translated, and read at the head of the armies who were fighting the battles of freedom. The writer of this book had the pleasure to receive in South America, while the independence of the new republics was as yet hardly established, the warmest evidences of the friendship of these new republicans for their North American brethren. This feeling of gratitude was mainly owing to the speeches of Henry Clay, which were accepted among the people as the sentiments of his countrymen. So far can one voice reach, when it is raised in defence of the right!

In 1827, General Bolivar sent a letter to Henry Clay, expressing in behalf of the South American people, whom he represented, the strongest feelings of gratitude. Mr. Clay, in answer, expressed his gratification that the course pursued by the government of the United States, had called forth such grateful sentiments. He added, moreover, with becoming frankness, a hope that certain imputations of ambitious designs to General Bolivar, would prove unfounded. Events afterward exonerated the South American Patriot.

CHAPTER XIV.

CLOSE OF THE FOURTEENTH CONGRESS — ITS LEADING
MEASURES — THE COMPENSATION ACT — PUBLIC DISSA-
TISFACTION — OPENING OF THE FIFTEENTH CONGRESS—
INTERNAL IMPROVEMENTS.

AT the close of the second session of the fourteenth Congress, Mr. Clay was complimented
with an unanimous vote of thanks, "for the
ability and impartiality with which he had presided over its deliberations, and the correctness
with which he had performed the arduous duties
of the chair." Such a resolution as this is a
matter of course under ordinary circumstances;
but the heartiness with which it was bestowed on
this occasion, gave it more than a mere complimentary character. The nature of the measures
which the House had been called upon to discuss,
added to the difficulties of the Speaker's position.
In making his acknowledgments, Mr. Clay remarked that there were in legislation three periods

of extraordinary difficulty, and requiring great fortitude. The first was that which immediately precedes a war, and in which preparation is made for that event; the second, that which accompanies, and the third, that which follows, war. During the two first, however, there were animating circumstances, always existing, which invigorated the legislative function. During the last, the stimulus is gone; and being succeeded by relaxation, the legislator needs more fortitude. He has to survey the whole fabric of the State, to accommodate it to the new circumstances in which it is placed; to provide a revenue for redeeming the debt of the war; to retrench, and by the reduction of establishments, to dismiss from the service of the country many who have nobly contributed to sustain its glory. In the latter of the three periods, Mr. Clay remarked, the members of the House whose term was just closing had been placed, and he reciprocated the compliment which the members had paid to him, by testifying to the patience, diligence, and zeal, which they had manifested in the public service.

Many public acts of much importance were passed. The system of coast defence received its first important aid at this session; the principle

of protection of American industry was recognised; a bill appropriating certain moneys to
internal improvements passed Congress, but was
vetoed by President Madison; the United States
Bank was chartered; but no public measure produced so much clamor as what was termed the
"Compensation Act."

Previous to this time, the pay of members of
Congress had been six dollars a day. A bill was
passed, giving to each member fifteen hundred
dollars per annum, without regard to the length
of the sessions. This law produced a great excitement, and was condemned, not only by popular meetings and the newspapers, but by formal
resolution in many of the State Legislatures. In
consequence of this it was repealed — the repeal
to take effect with the next Congress. The
members of the Congress which had passed the
law, in repealing it, made this compromise with
their dignity, that they permitted it to stand so
far as they were concerned. The next Congress,
we may here observe, passed the act affixing the
present rate—eight dollars per day and mileage;
and experience has demonstrated that the fifteen
hundred dollars per annum would have been a
much less tax on the public treasury.

13*

As the election for the new Congress took place before the act could be repealed, many members lost their seats. Some declined to be candidates for a re-election. Those who were re-elected came in by a very close vote. Even Mr. Clay was taught how much the popularity of a politician depends upon a breath. While his election was pending, and the popular clamor was at its height, he met an old Kentucky friend who showed ominous discontent on account of the charge of compensation which the members of Congress had voted to themselves.

"Have you a good rifle?" asked Mr. Clay.

"Yes."

"Did it never flash?"

"It did once."

"And did you then throw it away?"

"No; I picked the flint, and tried it again, and it was true."

"And will you throw me away?"

"No, no," said the hunter, grasping his hand, "I will pick the flint, and try it again!"

Mr. Clay was again elected Speaker of the House, in 1817, by a vote of one hundred and forty to seven. The measure with which he was most closely identified, during this session of Congress, was the passage of a resolution by the House, declaring that Congress has power, under the Constitution, to make appropriations for the construction of military roads, post roads, and canals. It passed the House by a vote of ninety to seventy-five. It is proper to say, however, that the question still remains open; and though large appropriations have been made from year to year for the improvement of river navigation, and the security of harbors, yet the construction of roads or canals, by the Federal Government, has never been reduced to a governmental system, as was contemplated by the originators of the policy.

Mr. Madison, as we have already said, vetoed a bill having internal improvements for its object. Mr. Monroe declared his opinion against the constitutional power of Congress, in his first message; and it was to meet the arguments of the message that the resolution above mentioned was introduced. It was at one time very common to suggest revisions and amendments of the Constitution, to meet particular exigencies. Thus Mr. Jefferson contemplated an amendment of the Constitution, to legalise the purchase of Louisiana. Madison and Monroe, while they opposed internal improvements by the Federal Government as unconstitutional, favored the policy, and wished the Constitution amended in order to permit it. But altering the fundamental law of a state or a confederacy is a doubtful experiment, and never to be resorted to except from imperious necessity. It is better to endure some evils and inconveniences, than to open the door to innovations which may amount to revolution, and which must impair the feeling of confidence and stability. The reasoning which Mr. Clay used against the probability of amending the Constitution in reference to internal improvements, will apply to such a proposal if entertained with any other view. " With regard," he said, " to the possibility of obtaining such an amendment, I think it altogether out of the question. Two different descriptions of persons, entertaining sentiments directly opposed, will unite and defeat such an amendment: one embracing those who believe that the Constitution, fairly interpreted, conveys the power; and the other, those who think that Congress has not, and ought not to have it."

Mr. Clay argued : " Of all the modes in which a government can employ its surplus revenue, none is more permanently beneficial than that of internal improvement. Fixed to the soil, it becomes a durable part of the land itself, diffusing comfort, and activity, and animation, on all sides. The first direct effect is on the agricultural community, into whose pockets comes the difference in the expense of transportation between good and bad ways. Thus, if the price of transporting a barrel of flour, by the erection of the Cumberland Turnpike, should be lessened two dollars, the producer of the article would receive that two dollars more now than formerly. But putting aside all pecuniary considerations, there may be political motives sufficiently powerful alone to justify certain improvements."

The "Cumberland Road" extends from Cumberland, Maryland, over the Alleghanies to Wheeling, Virginia. It was built by successive appropriations, commencing in 1806, and amounting in all to about two millions of dollars, exclusive of sums appropriated for surveys 600 miles further. This expense has been charged directly or indirectly upon the public lands. Superior modes of facilitating the transit of merchandise and passengers, have superseded turnpikes as objects of public patronage; and convenience, or policy, has transferred the erection or fostering of these works from the National to the State governments. Individual enterprise has proved more efficient than either; and the great branches of iron roads and water communication, which are spreading their arms in all directions, more than realise the predictions of Mr. Clay as to the advantage and benefits of internal improvements. The distant members of the confederacy are united; communication is between the principal points literally *instantaneous*, for the telegraph has been introduced to perfect the work which the Cumberland Road began, and may finally stretch across America from ocean to ocean.

Though we have said that the question as to the power of Congress to make appropriations for internal improvements still remains open, it is adjusted to a great extent by the disposition to compromise, which indeed determines, sooner or later, all our great national questions. Individuals originate, State legislatures aid or assume, and Congress by grants of land, or the proceeds of land sales, assists in uniting our country by the most magnificent public works ever erected. For rivers and harbors, and other public objects not of a nature to support themselves by the production of a revenue, Congress makes annual appropriations.

To Mr. Clay the country owes much of this prosperity. He saw the importance of easy and rapid inter-communication; and he advocated the government aid which gave the system its early impetus. Neither he, nor his compatriots, the opponents of the policy which he advocated, could foresee that the private energy of the people, aided by the discoveries of the age, would accomplish such wonders in art and enterprise as have now become common-place events. They could not predict that turnpikes, canals, and post roads, would be rendered obsolete by the railroad and the telegraph. But Mr. Clay's speeches in favor of internal improvement, if they did not effect all that he desired in the national councils, reached the ears of the people, and influenced the State legislatures. As the man in his strength does not forget the kindness which supported his childhood, so may Mr. Clay's countrymen — who are now driven by steam over the difficulties which once still farther impeded the ancient slow modes of conveyance — thank him who defended in its infancy the policy and enterprise which can now defend and sustain themselves.

CHAPTER XV.

THE relations of the United States with Spain
— embarrassed by the aid which the revolted
colonies, now the Spanish-American republics,
received from citizens of the United States —
were still farther complicated by the proceedings
of General Jackson, in the Seminole campaign of
1817. Sheltered within the Spanish territory of
Florida, the Seminole Indians committed great
depredations upon the frontier settlements of
Georgia. A few skirmishes took place between
the Indians and the American garrison of Fort
Scott, under the command of General Gaines.
Some lives were lost, and an Indian town was
surprised and burned. Up to this time, there
had been no invasion of the Spanish territory.

The Indians retaliated by capturing a boat, which was on its way up the Apalachicola River with supplies for Fort Scott. Between forty and fifty men, women, and children, were killed, and the United States Government took immediate steps to punish the Indians, and put a close to the state of Indian warfare. Major-General Andrew Jackson was ordered to take the command in person, and authority was conferred to enter Florida, if necessary, in pursuit of the Indians; but the instructions did not authorise an attack upon any Spanish fort.

General Jackson, with a large force, as promptly as the nature of the country and the insufficiency of supplies would permit, overran Florida, burned several Indian towns, and took possession of the Spanish post of St. Marks. The only resistance offered by the Spanish commander was a remonstrance. One of the Indian settlements, a town on the Suwanee River, received notice of his approach from Arbuthnot, an Indian trader. The women and children were sent away, and the warriors made a stand under the command of Ambrister, another Indian trader. The leader, Ambrister, was taken prisoner; the

14

other Englishman, Arbuthnot, had already been found in the fort at St. Marks.

Both these men were put on trial before a Court Martial, of which General Gaines was President; and both were found guilty of exciting the Indians to war, and furnishing them with supplies. Both were sentenced to death; and although, on re-consideration, the Court Martial changed Ambrister's sentence to stripes and imprisonment, General Jackson approved the first finding in the case of Ambrister, and caused the sentence of death to be put in execution upon both. Two Indian chiefs, who came on board an American armed vessel, which wore the British flag for a decoy, were also hanged by General Jackson's orders. Pensacola was taken possession of, and the aggressions of the Indians, and their shelter by the Spanish authorities, were thus summarily closed.

These measures called forth a protest from the Spanish Minister at Washington. John Quincy Adams, the Secretary of State, defended the invasion of Florida, on the ground that Spain had not fulfilled her treaty stipulations to keep the Indians in check. He justified the seizure of the Spanish posts as a measure of self-defence;

but as the war with the Indians was now ended, the forts taken were restored to the Spanish authorities.

It is matter of record that Adams was the only one in the Cabinet who defended General Jackson. That officer had acted on his own responsibility, and transcended the limit prescribed to him. But it was necessary to defend his course, on account of the position of the United States Government toward Spain, and because, as Mr. Madison said in a private letter to General Jackson, "the President was satisfied that General Jackson had good reason for his conduct, and had acted in all things on that principle." The people of the United States, having since given General Jackson the highest proofs of their confidence, may be regarded as excusing him, under the circumstances, for acts the principle of which would have justified the British forces in Canada in invading our northern frontier, during the Canadian rebellion. Perhaps the failure of our government to disavow General Jackson's course, or to censure him, may account for the omission of any demand, on our part, for reparation for the burning of an American steamboat by a British party, while she was moored in the waters of the United States. What a nation exacts, she must endure; and if General Jackson was defended in taking possession of Spanish forts, because they were thought to shield hostile Indians, the same plea of self-defence would be available in justification of the destruction of a steamboat in the service of an enemy; though that steamer had taken refuge in the waters of a friendly power.

Whatever may be said of General Jackson's Florida proceedings at this day, when party feelings enter no more into the estimate, we must concede that the most friendly disposition can only palliate, and not commend them. At the time of their occurrence, there was a strong disposition to call the General to an account. Mr. Adams saved him in the Cabinet; and, once committed, the administration was forced to defend him. The documents relative to the Seminole war, and the Spanish protest, were laid before the House of Representatives, and referred to the Committee on Naval Affairs. In their report, the seizure and occupation of the Spanish posts was condemned; and to the report a series of resolutions was appended. Among them was one expressive of censure on General Jackson for the execution of Arbuthnot and Ambrister. There was a minority report which defended General Jackson for the occupation of the Spanish towns. The debate lasted three weeks; and resulted in a refusal to censure General Jackson, by a majority of between thirty and forty votes.

Many very able speeches were made — none more able than the speeches of Henry Clay. The whole subject was reviewed by him. In his opening, he disclaimed all feelings towards General Jackson but those of kindness and respect. He reviewed and condemned the Indian Treaty made four years before, the hard terms of which, he alleged, produced this war. He condemned in eloquent language, the execution of the Indians, and that of the Englishmen, without, as he urged, the authority of law. It is not our purpose now to revive the charges against General Jackson; and we pass, therefore, the particular points which Mr. Clay made, and extract the more general conclusion of his speech; sound in wisdom, and earnest in patriotism.

"I will not," said Mr. Clay, "trespass much longer upon the time of the Committee; but I trust I shall be indulged in some few reflections upon the danger of permitting the conduct on

14*

which it has been my painful duty to animadvert, to pass without a solemn expression of the disapprobation of this House. Recall to your recollection the free nations which have gone before us. Where are they now?

Some glimmering through the dream of things that were,
A school-boy's tale, the wonder of an hour.

And how have they lost their liberties? If we could transport ourselves back to the ages when Greece and Rome flourished in their greatest prosperity, and, mingling in the throng, should ask a Grecian if he did not fear that some daring military chieftain, covered with glory—some Philip or Alexander—would one day overthrow the liberties of his country, the confident and indignant Grecian would exclaim, 'No! no! we have nothing to fear from our heroes; our liberties will be eternal.' If a Roman citizen had been asked if he did not fear that the conqueror of Gaul might establish a throne upon the ruins of public liberty, he would instantly have repelled the insinuation. Yet Greece fell. Cæsar passed the Rubicon, and even the patriotic arm of Brutus could not preserve the liberties of his devoted country! The celebrated Madame de Stael, in her last, and perhaps her best work, has said, that in the very year, almost in the very month, when the president of the Directory declared that monarchy would never more show its frightful head in France, Bonaparte, with his grenadiers, entered the palace of St. Cloud, and dispersing with the bayonet the deputies of the people, deliberating on the affairs of the State, laid the foundation of that vast fabric of despotism which overshadowed all Europe. I hope not to be misunderstood. I am far from intimating that General Jackson cherishes any designs inimical to the liberties of the country. I believe his intentions to be pure and patriotic. I thank Heaven that he would not — and I am still more grateful that he could not if he would—overturn the liberties of the republic. But precedents, if bad, are fraught with the most dangerous consequences. Man has been described, by some one of those who have treated of his nature, as a bundle of habits. The definition is much truer when applied to governments. Precedents are their habits. There is one important difference between the formation of habits by an individual and by governments. He contracts it only after frequent repetition. A single instance fixes the habits and determines the direction of governments. Against the alarming doctrine of unlimited discretion in our military commanders, when applied even to prisoners of war, I must enter my protest. It begins with them — it will end on us. I hope our happy form of government is to be perpetuated. But if it is to be preserved, it must be by the practice of virtue, by justice, by moderation, by magnanimity, by greatness of soul, by keeping a watchful and steady eye on the executive; and, above all, by holding to a strict accountability the military branch of the public force.

" We are fighting a great moral battle, for the benefit not only of our country, but of all mankind. The eyes of the whole world are in fixed attention upon us. One, and the largest portion, is gazing with contempt, with jealousy, and with envy; the other portion with hope, with confidence, and with affection. Every where the thick cloud of legitimacy is suspended over the world, save only one bright spot, which breaks out from the political hemisphere of the West, to enlighten, and animate, and gladden the human heart. Obscure that, by the downfall of liberty here, and all mankind are enshrouded in a pall of universal darkness. To you, Mr. Chairman, belongs the high privilege of transmitting unimpaired, to posterity, the fair character and liberty of our country. Do you expect to execute this high trust by trampling, or suffering to be trampled down, law, justice, the constitution, and the rights of the people? by exhibiting examples of inhumanity, and cruelty, and ambition? When the minions of despotism heard, in Europe, of the seizure of Pensacola, how did they chuckle, and chide the admirers of our institutions, tauntingly pointing to the demonstration of a spirit of injustice and aggrandizement made by our country in the midst of an amicable negotiation. Behold, said they, the conduct of those who are constantly reproaching kings! You saw how those admirers were astounded, and hung their heads. You saw, too, when that illustrious man who presides over us adopted his pacific, moderate, and just course, how they once more lifted up their heads, with exultation and delight beaming in their countenances. And you saw how those minions themselves were fully compelled to unite in the general praises bestowed upon our government. Beware how you forfeit this exalted character. Beware how you give a fatal sanction, in this infant period of our republic, scarcely yet two

score years old, to military insubordination
Remember that Greece had her Alexander, Rome
her Cæsar, England her Cromwell, France her
Bonaparte; and that if we would escape the rock
on which they split, we must avoid their errors.

"I hope gentlemen will deliberately survey the
awful isthmus on which we stand. They may
bear down all opposition; they may even vote
the General the public thanks; they may carry
him triumphantly through this House. But if
they do, in my humble judgment, it will be a
triumph of the principle of insubordination — a
triumph of the military over the civil authority
— a triumph over the powers of this House — a
triumph over the constitution of the land. And
I pray most devoutly to Heaven, that it may not
prove, in its ultimate effects and consequences, a
triumph over the liberties of the people."

CHAPTER XVI.

THE MISSOURI COMPROMISE — RETIREMENT OF MR. CLAY
— HIS MISSION TO VIRGINIA — VISIT TO HANOVER —
SPEECH BEFORE THE VIRGINIA HOUSE OF DELEGATES.

THE next important measure in which we find
Mr. Clay engaged, was the famous "Missouri
Compromise." Before the admission of a new
State into the Union, an Act of Congress is required to authorise a convention of the people to
form a constitution. In the session of 1818–19,
the House passed such an act for the State of
Missouri. But it contained a proviso forbidding
the farther introduction of slavery into the new
State, and providing that all slaves born in the
State after its admission into the Union, should
be free at the age of twenty-five. The Senate
refused to pass the bill with these provisions, and
the session went over with the appeal of Missouri still unanswered.

At the next session, the matter came up again.

There was a long and very warm debate upon the subject. As the "Missouri Compromise" is a phrase which our young readers will often meet, it may be well to make it intelligible to them. In 1787, while the States were as yet united simply by articles of confederation, an ordinance was unanimously agreed to, for the government of the territory north-west of the Ohio. This ordinance, among other provisions, declared that "there shall be neither slavery nor involuntary servitude in the said territory, otherwise than the punishment of crimes, whereof the party shall have been duly convicted." This provision had been strictly adhered to, up to the date of the application of Missouri for admission.

Prior to 1820, when the Missouri question was settled, ten States had been added to the original thirteen. Among these were: Vermont, separated from New York, and Maine from Massachusetts, States in which slavery was not mentioned; Ohio, Indiana, and Illinois, from the territory north and west of the Ohio. By the constitutions of the last three States, slavery was expressly excluded, in accordance with the terms of the ordinance above mentioned. To balance these five free States, Tennessee, from North

Carolina, Kentucky, from Virginia; Louisiana, from the Louisiana purchase; and Mississippi and Alabama from lands ceded to the United States by Georgia, had been admitted into the Union. In these States, slavery had not been forbidden, as they formed portions of territory formerly held by slave States; and occupied, so far as settled, by slave-holders.

The State of Missouri was formed out of part of the Louisiana purchase; and it was contended that the new State should follow the precedents of the other States which had been created out of slave territory. Louisiana had slaves, and as Missouri was another portion of the same purchase, it was demanded that she should be received on the same footing as a slave-holding State. The argument had weight, independent of any question as to slavery, from its merits or demerits as a separate question. If any State, under the Constitution and the precedents established, was entitled to hold slaves, Missouri held that right; since the French province of Louisiana, of which her territory formed a part, recognised slavery.

The dispute was adjusted, at length, by admitting Missouri as a slave State, with a proviso that in all the territory ceded to the United States by France, north of latitude thirty six degrees, thirty minutes, slavery shall not exist; the limits of Missouri of course being excepted. This proviso or compromise, together with the ordinance of 1787, includes the whole western territory. Some of the thirteen States which ceded their lands to the United States, claimed to hold to the Pacific; but their limits were very vague. So also were the limits of Louisiana, but the " Missouri Compromise" renders it now unnecessary to determine whether territory from which new States may be formed, belonged to the Louisiana grant, or was part of the domain of the "Old Thirteen." The line of latitude defines the limit. The accessions from Mexico open a new question; but of these, Texas was certainly a part of the tract sold to the United States by Napoleon. It was ceded to Spain by the treaty of 1821, in which Florida was acquired; and perhaps some of our readers may remember to have heard the admission of Texas into the Union, termed a "re-annexation."

To effect this compromise, Mr. Clay labored with all his powers of argument and of conciliation. But the matter was not here settled. At the next session, that of 1820–21, the difficulty presented itself in a new form. Missouri had adopted her Constitution, and came with it to Washington, to be formally admitted. But the instrument contained a provision which re-awakened all the bitterness of the contest. It was in these words: "It shall be the duty of the General Assembly, as soon as may be, to pass such laws as may be necessary to prevent free negroes and mulattoes from coming to, and settling in this State, under any pretext whatever." The Senate passed a resolution admitting the State of Missouri — but the House refused to admit the new State with such a provision in its Constitution. Meanwhile, the ceremony of counting the electoral votes, as directed by the Constitution of the United States, must take place in the presence of the Senate and House of Representatives. The expedient was resorted to of declaring the vote first *with* that of Missouri, and then *without* it, to show that the vote of the suspended state did not alter the result. But when the vote of Missouri was reached, terrific confusion arose. Some cried, " Missouri is a State !" and others, " Missouri is not a State !" The Senate withdrew from the disturbance; motion after motion was made, and rejected. Mr. Clay, at last, persuaded his fellow-members into a momentary calm, and made a motion that the Senate be notified that the House was now ready to complete the duty of counting the votes. The Senate returned; the rest of the States were counted, and it was declared that President Monroe was re-elected, by a vote of 231 *with*, and 228 *without* Missouri. Mr. Randolph, and others, attempted to throw some doubts on the legality of the proceeding, but that point was abandoned.

It was during this session that Mr. Clay received the title of the Great Pacificator. He had resigned his office as Speaker, on account of his inability to attend at the opening of the session; and he reached Washington when the House was in the midst of confusion, and all public business was defeated by this vexed question. Twice he procured the appointment of a committee, to which the resolution to admit Missouri was referred. The report of the first committee was rejected. The second committee consisted of twenty-three members — one from each State — with Mr. Clay as chairman, to meet a joint-committee of the Senate. Their unanimous report was a resolution by which Missouri was admitted, on condition of her removing the obnoxious clause. It was carried in both Houses, and the new State accepted the terms. Thus passed away what had been a serious and alarming cause of anxiety. This pacific result, as well as others which he has accomplished, Mr. Clay produced as much by personal appeals, and individual applications, as by his public speeches. He left no mode or effort of conciliation untried, and spared himself no labor.

At the close of this session of Congress, Mr. Clay retired, as he supposed, from public life. He had become embarrassed in his pecuniary relations by the misfortunes of a friend for whom he had endorsed; and desired, by resuming the practice of his profession, to retrieve his affairs. There was now a season of repose in the national councils. The House, at this session, approved Mr. Clay's policy in reference to the South American republics, as developed in his frequent speeches, by passing a resolution that they were ready to second the President, whenever he should deem it advisable to recognise their independence. The treaty with Spain, now ratified, removed all danger of collision with that power, by the acquisition of Florida and the cession of

15*

Texas; thus cancelling all foreign governments east of the Mississippi, and accurately defining our limits on the west.

But although Mr. Clay resigned his seat in the National Legislature with a view to private life, his fellow-citizens could not forego his important public services. He was appointed in 1821, in connection with Mr. Bibb, to adjust certain conflicting land claims with the State of Virginia. Through the loose manner in which Virginia had disposed of her public lands before Kentucky was erected into a State, land-titles in Kentucky were often insecure. The Legislature of Kentucky had passed a law by which, though a resident was dispossessed by the proof of a prior title, the claimant should pay for the permanent improvements. The principle of this law was contested, and the Supreme Court of the United States decided against it. Mr. Clay's mission was to procure, from the Legislature of Virginia, some arrangement by which this difficulty could be avoided. The result was the appointment of commissioners—Hon. B. W. Leigh on the part of Virginia, and Mr. Clay on the part of Kentucky. Their labors were only in part successful; but the service in which Mr. Clay was employed was

one of the proudest rewards of his early application and industry.

The poor boy, who left Virginia thirty years
before to seek his fortune, now returned to Richmond, the scene of his early struggles, the
honored representative of a sister State. He
brought with him the character of a profound
lawyer, an accomplished legislator, an able diplo-
matist, and a powerful orator. His reputation
preceded him in all that he undertook, and the
prestige of his name was almost the assurance of
success. As may readily be supposed, his presence in Richmond, and the knowledge of his
mission, attracted a large concourse of people.
Mr. Clay found it one of the most trying occasions of his life. On the way to Richmond he
had visited the "Slashes"—the grave of his
father, the scenes of his childhood; and the visit
had re-awakened in his mind the memories of
other years, and the feelings with which he had
left his home to become a pioneer in the comparative wilderness of Kentucky.

The hall of the delegates was crowded on the
day of the appearance of Mr. Clay before them.
There he saw all who survived of the old men
who were in their prime in his boyhood, and who

befriended his youth.   He met on terms of more
than equality, the representatives of the families
to association with whom the shop-boy could
hardly have dared to hope.   He found himself
in the presence of an auditory distinguished for
culture and intellect; and he was under the influence of emotions which must either entirely
enervate him, or raise him above himself.

But he was equal to the occasion.   He depicted, in language flowing from a feeling heart,
the misfortunes of those — his neighbors and
friends — whose case he had come to plead.   He
described the pioneer crossing the Alleghanies,
with no possession save his stout heart and strong
arm.   He painted the perils from wild beasts and
savage men; he described the reward, in the
results of fortitude, courage, and patient industry.
He brought forward the picture of the lord of
the soil, rich in the earnings of his own hands
—happy in his domestic relations—looking with
complacency on the inheritance he could devise
to his children — then suddenly reversing the
picture, described his ejectment that another
might reap the reward of his labors.   The picture of disappointment and unhappiness which

he drew moved his audience almost to tears — nor was the speaker unaffected. Henry Clay was no actor, and counterfeited no emotion which he did not feel; and he never was so eloquent as when advocating the cause of the oppressed or the unfortunate. His old friends heard with their own ears, the evidence that their expectations relative to the Mill-Boy of the Slashes, had not been disappointed.

CHAPTER XVII.

AFTER nearly three years' absence from Congress, Mr. Clay was persuaded to re-enter the House. He was elected without opposition, and was, as before, chosen to the Speakership; receiving 139 votes, against 40, which were cast for Mr. Barbour, of Virginia, the late Speaker. In taking the Chair, he made, as was his custom, some pertinent remarks.

At this session, Mr. Clay's love of freedom had a new channel for its exercise. The independence of the South American republics had been formally acknowledged, at the suggestion of the President, during Mr. Clay's absence from Congress. Daniel Webster brought forward a resolution that provision should be made for the appointment of a commissioner to Greece. Mr. Clay heartily supported this resolution. President Monroe had referred to the condition of Greece, then struggling for liberty, in two annual messages; but had made no suggestion relative to action. The following are extracts from the speech of Mr. Clay, while the subject was under debate:

"Mr. Chairman, is it not extraordinary that for these two successive years, the President of the United States should have been freely indulged, not only without censure, but with universal approbation, to express the feelings which the resolution proclaims, and yet, if this House venture to unite with him, the most awful consequences are to ensue? From Maine to Georgia, and from the Atlantic Ocean to the Gulf of Mexico, the sentiment of approbation has blazed with the rapidity of electricity. Everywhere the interest in the Grecian cause is felt with the deepest intensity, expressed in every form, and increases with every new day and passing hour. And are the representatives of the people alone to be insulated from the common moral atmosphere of the whole land? Shall we shut ourselves up in apathy, and separate ourselves from our country, from our constituents, from our Chief Magistrate, from our principles?

"The measure has been most unreasonably magnified. Gentlemen speak of the watchful jealousy of the Turk, and seem to think the slightest movement of this body will be matter of serious speculation at Constantinople. I believe that neither the Sublime Porte, nor the European allies, attach any such exaggerated importance to the acts and deliberations of this body. The Turk will, in all probability, never hear the names of the gentlemen who either espouse or oppose the resolution. It certainly is not without a value; but that value is altogether moral.

"Are we so mean, so base, so despicable, that we may not attempt to express our horror, utter our indignation, at the most brutal and atrocious war that ever stained earth, or shocked high Heaven? at the ferocious deeds of a savage and infuriated soldiery, stimulated and urged on by the priests of a fanatical and inimical religion, and rioting in all the extremes of blood and butchery—at the mere details of which the heart sickens and recoils?

"If the great body of Christendom can look on so calmly and coolly, while all this is perpetrated on a Christian people in its own immediate vicinity — in its very presence — let us at least evince, that one of its remote extremities is susceptible of sensibility to Christian wrongs, and capable of sympathy for Christian sufferings; that in this remote quarter of the world, there are hearts not yet closed against compassion for human woes; that can pour out their indignant feelings at the oppression of a people endeared to us by every ancient recollection, and by every modern tie. Sir, attempts have been made to alarm the committee by the dangers to our commerce in the Mediterranean; and a wretched invoice of figs and opium has been spread before us, to repress our sensibilities, and to eradicate our humanity. Ah, Sir, 'what shall it profit a man if he gain the whole world, and lose his own soul?' or what shall it avail a nation to save the whole of a miserable trade, and lose its liberties?

The resolution, though moved by Mr. Webster, and defended with so much zeal and eloquence by Mr. Clay, did not pass. But we may add here, to save future reference to the same theme, that during the administration of John Q. Adams, while Henry Clay was Secretary of State, the independence of Greece was recognised, (the United States being the first nation to render the

16

classic land this justice) and a Minister was sent
to Greece.

In 1824, General Lafayette arrived in this
country — the nation's guest. Congress had
passed a resolution placing a national vessel at
his service, but he, with characteristic modesty,
preferred to come in a packet-ship. He landed
at Castle Garden, New York, on the 16th of
August; and was received with demonstrations
of respect, gratitude, and affection, which wel-
comed and attended him wherever he appeared
in the United States. It is not within our scope
to recount the incidents of his progress, but his
reception by the House of Representatives is a
part of the narrative of the life of Henry Clay.
Upon him, as Speaker of the House, devolved
the duty of welcoming the distinguished friend
of his country; and he performed that grateful
office in the following words:

"General — the House of Representatives of
the United States, impelled alike by its own
feelings, and by those of the whole American
people, could not have assigned to me a more
pleasant duty, than that of being its organ to
present to you cordial congratulations upon the
occasion of your recent arrival in the United

States, in compliance with the wishes of Congress, and to assure you of the very high satisfaction which your presence affords on this early theatre of your glory and renown. Although but few of the members which compose this body, shared with you in the war of the Revolution, all have a knowledge — from impartial history or from faithful tradition — of the perils, the sufferings, and the sacrifices which you have voluntarily encountered, and the signal services in America and in Europe, which you performed for an in-fant, a distant, and an alien people; and all feel and own the great extent of obligations under which you have placed our country. But the relations in which you have ever stood to the United States, interesting and important as they have ever been, do not constitute the only motive of the respect and admiration which this House entertains for you. Your consistency of charac-ter, your uniform devotion to regulated liberty in all the vicissitudes of a long and arduous life, also command its highest admiration. During all the recent convulsions of Europe, amidst, as after the dispersion of every political storm, the people of the United States have ever beheld you true to your old principles, firm and erect, cheer-

ing and animating, with your well-known voice,
the votaries of liberty; its faithful and fearless
champion, ready to shed the last drop of that
blood, which here you so freely and nobly shed
in the same holy cause.

"The vain wish has been sometimes indulged,
that Providence would allow the patriot, after
death, to return to his country, and to contemplate the intermediate changes which had taken
place — to view the forests felled, the cities built,
the mountains levelled, the canals cut, the high-
ways constructed, the progress of the arts, the
advancement of learning, and the increase of
population. General, your present visit to the
United States is the realisation of the consoling
object of that wish. You are in the midst of
posterity! Everywhere you must have been
struck with the great changes, physical and moral,
which have occurred since you left us. Even this
very city, bearing a venerated name alike endeared to you and to us, has since emerged from
the forest which then covered its site. In one
respect you behold us unaltered, and that is in
this sentiment of continued devotion to liberty,
and of ardent affection and profound gratitude to
your departed friend, the father of his country,

and to your illustrious associates in the field and in the cabinet, for the multiplied blessings which surround us, and for the very privilege of addressing you, which I now exercise. This sentiment, now fondly cherished by more than ten millions of people, will be transmitted, with unabated vigor, down the tide of time, through the countless millions who are destined to inhabit this continent, to the latest posterity."

To this address, General Lafayette made a graceful and grateful reply. He was afterward Mr. Clay's guest at Ashland; and while the distinguished Frenchman lived, he entertained for the American statesman a respect which rose to admiration, and a friendship which had the warmth of affection. "That is the man whom I hope to see President of the United States," said Lafayette in 1832 — pointing to a portrait of Henry Clay, which hung in his country-house. But it was a hope in which thousands of the admirers of the great statesman were disappointed.

16*

CHAPTER XVIII.

ELECTION OF J. Q. ADAMS — HIS TESTIMONY TO MR. CLAY
—MR. CLAY IN THE CABINET—THE PANAMA MISSION—
MR. RANDOLPH AND MR. CLAY—THEIR LAST INTERVIEW.

In 1825, John Quincy Adams commenced his administration, with Henry Clay as his Secretary of State. There were four candidates for the office of President — Andrew Jackson, who had ninety-nine votes; John Quincy Adams, eighty-four; William H. Crawford, forty-one; and Henry Clay, thirty-seven. By the Constitution of the United States, when there is a failure to elect a President by the votes of the electors, the House of Representatives designate one of the three highest candidates. Mr. Clay was thus ruled out, being the lowest in number, of four. As a member of the House of Representatives, he gave his vote to John Quincy Adams. The mode of election in the House of Representatives is by States. Adams received the votes of thir-

teen States, Jackson of seven, and Crawford of
four. We shall not need here to disprove the
charge made against Mr. Clay, that there was a
bargain between him and Mr. Adams, by which
he gave Mr. Adams his support, and received in
return the office of Secretary. It is sufficient to
say that the charge, having served its temporary
electioneering purposes, has been abundantly dis-
proved, and of late years forgotten. Mr. Adams
has, on more than one occasion, solemnly proclaimed the charge false; and we find him in
reference to it using the following language, not
more emphatic than it is just:

"As to my motives for tendering to him the
department of State when I did, let that man
who questions them come forward. Let him
look round among statesmen and legislators of
this nation, and of that day. Let him then select
and name the man whom, by his pre-eminent
talents, by his splendid services, by his ardent
patriotism, by his all-embracing public spirit, by
his fervid eloquence in behalf of the rights and
liberties of mankind, by his long experience in
the affairs of the Union, foreign and domestic, a
President of the United States, intent only upon
the honor and welfare of his country, ought to

have preferred to Henry Clay. Let him name that man, and then judge you, fellow-citizens, of my motives."

Mr. Clay justified the wisdom of Mr. Adams in his choice. We may remark that Mr. Adams also invited Mr. Crawford into his cabinet, but that gentleman did not accept. Had he seen fit to take place under Mr. Adams, the rare spectacle would have been presented of three men, whom citizens of the United States deemed competent to sit in the Executive chair, occupying the high places of the government together. Mr. Adams's administration, so far as the distribution of office was concerned, was eminently national, and not partisan. He did nothing to procure his re-nomination, or to continue himself in office. His measures were marked by independence in his domestic administration, and by manliness in his foreign intercourse. The stamp of Mr. Clay's policy was upon all the measures upon which he was consulted, or which legitimately fell within his department; and he proved no less efficient as a Cabinet Minister, than he had been as a Representative of the people in Congress. Wherever he was placed, he was always a leader; for his mighty mind commanded pre-eminence. He followed up in his new sphere the leading measures of his life; preserving, in the treaties with foreign nations which he negotiated, his principles respecting American industry and true independence. Through the foreign diplomatic relations of the country, he found means to forward the recognition, by other powers, of South American and of Grecian independence.

In the year 1825, the Spanish-American Republics invited the United States · to meet, at Panama, delegates from those republics, to deliberate on measures for the promotion of union and mutual assistance. Messrs. John Sergeant and Richard C. Anderson were appointed agents on the part of the United States. Mr. Clay, as Secretary of State, furnished them with a letter of instructions. In this document, he defended the most philanthropic national policy in war, and the most liberal and enlightened measures in peace. All his diplomatic correspondence was worthy of the man and of the republic.

It is not to be supposed, however, that an administration coming into power against such exasperated opposition as Mr. Adams encountered, could escape detraction. The measures of government were freely canvassed in the Senate; and upon the Panama Mission, Mr. Randolph, who had now a seat in the Senate, commented with exceeding bitterness. His old exasperation against Mr. Clay seemed to have increased in rancor, and he used language in reference to the President and his Secretary of State, for which mental infirmity could alone be urged in extenuation. Unhappily, Mr. Clay was tempted to demand explanation or retraction. Mr. Randolph refused, and a hostile meeting followed. Thus a second time was Mr. Clay betrayed into the criminal folly of a duel. "It was a grievous fault," and Mr. Clay was made "grievously to answer it." There is no doubt, that more than anything else, the charge of being a duellist was effective against his hopes and prospects, in those portions of the United States where duelling is held in its proper detestation. The immediate cause of irritation in this case, was the application of an epithet to Mr. Clay by Randolph, which implied that he was a gambler. It was one of a long series of premeditated insults, intended, it is supposed, to provoke a duel; but which a man like Henry Clay should, in any case, have been above resenting.

We may here take occasion to say, that, in the manner in which Mr. Randolph applied the term used to Mr. Clay, it was unjust. There are in some parts of our country — or have been, for we hope the public mind is growing sounder upon the subject—certain conventional rules of society, which make games of chance a reputable amusement under certain circumstances. These rules Mr. Clay never transgressed, even in the days of his youth. He never played at a public table or in a gambling-house. Before Mr. Randolph made that charge, Mr. Clay had ceased to play at games of hazard. Yet, his political enemies succeeded at one time in producing an impression that he was what Mr. Randolph termed him. No man is perfect, and we claim no perfection for Henry Clay. But now that the earth covers his remains, we may defend his memory from unjust aspersions, while we do not conceal the truth, or deny the reader the warning which his example affords, that we should not only avoid evil, but "every appearance of evil."

The duel between Mr. Clay and Mr. Randolph was without any wound to either. As Mr. Randolph's name will not occur again in this book, this is a proper place to mention these last interviews. In 1833, a few weeks before Mr. Randolph's death, he came to the Senate chamber, being too ill to stand or walk without assistance. Mr. Clay had just risen to make some remarks. "Help me up," said Mr. Randolph to his half-brother, Mr. B. Tucker; "*I have come to hear that voice.*" Mr. Clay went to him as soon as he had concluded his remarks, and exchanged salutations. It is pleasant to hear that they were thus reconciled; the more especially that through their long official life, there had been so many causes of irritation between them. It was Mr. Clay's practice to avoid Mr. Randolph, when he knew that the eccentric man meditated an affront. But his situation as Speaker was one of peculiar difficulty, since, in enforcing order, he was compelled to cross the erratic gentleman's path, and occasionally to compel him to sit down. Mr. Clay, however, was always an impartial presiding officer; and it is related of him, that though for so many years Speaker of the House, there was seldom an appeal against his decisions; and during the latter years of his Speakership, no dispute with him upon points of order. Indeed, he may be said to have established the usage of the House in many particulars; and to have served his country as usefully in his sphere, as any other of her statesmen, or any of her warriors.

CHAPTER XIX.

MR. CLAY'S RETIREMENT — HIS ELECTION TO THE SENATE — REMOVAL OF THE DEPOSITES — EXPUNGING RESOLUTION — THE COMPROMISE TARIFF.

MR. CLAY'S health had suffered very much during his residence in Washington, and the close of his official position as Secretary of State was by no means unwelcome to him. A pleasant anecdote is related of his homeward journey. Twenty-five years ago there were none of the railroad facilities which now make travelling a pastime. It was a laborious and very fatiguing task to make long journeys. Mr. Clay was entering Uniontown, Pennsylvania, on an outside seat of the stage-coach, a place he had taken in preference to the inside. The citizens of Uniontown expressed some surprise at seeing the Ex-Secretary in that high and exposed situation. "Gentlemen," said Mr. Clay, "although I am with the *outs*, the *ins* behind me have much the worst of it!"

For two years Mr. Clay remained in retirement — if that life may be called retirement, the
quiet of which is frequently broken by the hospi-
talities of admiring friends. Wherever Mr. Clay
moved abroad, he met the warmest demonstrations of popular affection. His friends were
anxious to show their estimate of the unfounded
allegation of " bargain," which had been so successfully used against him; and not a few, probably, of his political opponents, were willing
enough to compliment the man in a way which
did not commit their votes, or advance his political prospects. He was pressed to accept a nomination to the Kentucky Legislature, and to the
House of Representatives, but declined both.

In 1831 the Kentucky Legislature elected him
to the Senate of the United States; and in the
same year Mr. Clay was a second time nominated
for the office of Presidency of the Union. We
may mention here the well-known result. General Jackson was in 1832 re-elected by a very
large majority, receiving 219 votes, and Henry
Clay 49. Eighteen votes were cast for John
Floyd and William Wirt. General Jackson was
at this time at the height of his prosperity. He
had refused his assent to the recharter of the

Bank of the United States, and his course in this respect proved eminently popular. Unfortunately for themselves as a party, the Whigs, as the supporters of Mr. Clay were called, made first the re-charter of the old bank, and afterward the establishment of a new one, a leading measure of their policy. The unprejudiced observer cannot do otherwise than confess, that among the consequences of the defeat of the Bank of the United States, and the failure of the State Bank, afterward chartered in Pennsylvania, and miscalled by the name of the old National Institution, is to be reckoned loss and defeat to the Whig party. In a previous chapter we have said all that our plan includes relative to the subject. We may here observe, that some of the most brilliant oratorical efforts of Mr. Clay during his later services in the Senate, were in opposition to President Jackson's financial measures. The withdrawal of the public money from the custody of the Bank of the United States, commonly spoken of as " the removal of the deposites," was an act the legality of which was strongly disputed ; and the Senate, 26 to 20, passed, in March, 1833, a resolution " that the President, in the late executive proceedings in relation to the public revenue, has assumed upon himself authority and power not conferred by the constitution and laws, but in derogation of both." This resolution was introduced and supported by Mr. Clay. The President sent a protest to the Senate against the resolution, which that body, by a vote of 27 to 16, refused to insert in the journal. By the same vote they declared that the President of the United States has no right to send a protest to the Senate against any of its proceedings. In January, 1836, a resolution was passed by the efforts of Mr. Benton, a warm personal friend of the President, by which this resolution of censure was cancelled or exchanged. The cancellation was done by drawing black lines around it, and Mr. Benton carried away the pen as a trophy. Through the whole of the debates to which Mr. Benton's resolution gave rise, Mr. Clay maintained his ground; but changes in the Senate had produced an effective majority for the measure.

This term of Mr. Clay's service in the Senate, from 1831 to 1837, was signalized by his great Tariff Compromise, the second of the three leading efforts of patriotism which distinguished his public career. The tariff of 1824, in support of which Mr. Clay made one of his most celebrated speeches, had now, as Mr. Clay and his friends contended, established the soundness of the protective policy, and elevated the business interests of the country and its general prosperity, to a position almost unexampled. In 1828, while Mr. Clay was Secretary of State, the tariff of 1824 was altered, and, against the judgment of Mr. Clay, made exceedingly obnoxious to the opponents of protection. These difficulties were, in some degree, afterward remedied, and the amended and re-amended tariff continued a short time longer. In 1831, the administration indicated an intention to alter this tariff, in order to reduce the revenue to the wants of government, for which, it was found, the customs were more than adequate. The opponents of the protective system were ready to seize the occasion to reduce the tariff, without regard to the principle of protection—or rather with a view to the destruction of the protective policy. Mr. Clay anticipated them by introducing a resolution, the purport of which was, that duties on articles imported from foreign countries, not coming in competition with American articles, ought forthwith to be abolished. As the resolution did not permit the leading principle of the system

17*

to be touched, it was vigorously opposed by the opponents of protection, and ably defended by Mr. Clay. A bill was reported in compliance with this resolution, and passed at the close of a long session. The act, as passed, was a triumph for Mr. Clay, as it preserved the great principle for which he had all his life contended.

The enemies of the protective system were not yet satisfied. The State of South Carolina, in particular, was exceedingly discontented, and the famous nullification measures of that State followed upon the tariff of 1831. President Jackson, on the 10th of December, 1832, issued his proclamation, announcing that the revenue laws must be enforced. Governor Hayne of South Carolina answered the President in a counter proclamation. A bill was brought forward in the United States House of Representatives, reducing the duties on all protected articles; and in the Senate, a bill to *enforce* the collection of the revenue, wherever opposition was offered.

It was a stormy crisis. Civil war seemed impending; for the hot spirits in South Carolina, who had threatened opposition to the Federal Government, seemed in danger of being forced by their own acts into collision; and none who knew the stern character of the President, doubted that he would employ all the means within his reach to enforce the laws of the Union, at whatever sacrifice. In this juncture, the House Tariff Bill still being pending, Mr. Clay brought forward his famous Compromise Tariff. The main feature of the bill was, that it provided for a gradual reduction of the Tariff until 1842, when a twenty per centum should be the rate of duties, until otherwise provided by law. It passed both Houses by quite a large majority, considering the state of parties, the vote being 120 to 84 in the House, and 29 to 16 in the Senate. The storm subsided: the country was quieted, and Mr. Clay stood proudly before his countrymen, as the man who had averted collision between a State and the Federal administration, and still maintained the principle of protection. There were not wanting some angry spirits who would have been glad to find the question of resistance brought to the test of force. To such Mr. Clay said:

"If there be any who want civil war, who want to see the blood of any portion of our countrymen spilt, I am not one of them. I wish to see war of no kind; but, above all, I do not desire to see a civil war. When war begins, whether civil or foreign, no human sight is competent to foresee when, or how, or where it is to terminate. But when a civil war shall be lighted up in the bosom of our own happy land, and enemies are marching, and commanders are winning their victories, and fleets are in motion on our coast, tell me, if you can, tell me if any human being can, tell its duration. God only knows where such a war would end. In what a state will our institutions be left? In what a state our liberties? I want no war; above all, no war at home.

"Sir, I repeat that I think South Carolina has been rash, intemperate and greatly in the wrong; but I do not want to disgrace her, or any other member of the Union. No: I do not want to see the lustre of one single star dimmed of our glorious confederacy; still less do I wish to see it blotted out, and its light obliterated for ever. Has not the State of South Carolina been one of the members of this Union in 'the times that tried men's souls?' Have not her ancestors fought along-side our ancestors? Have we not consequently won many a glorious battle? If we had to go into a civil war with such a State, how would it terminate? Whenever it should have terminated, what would be her condition? If she should ever return to the Union, what would be the condition of her feelings and affections?— what the state of the heart of her people? She has been with us before when her ancestors mingled in the throng of battle; and as I hope our posterity will mingle with hers, for centuries to come, in the united defence of liberty, and for the honor and glory of the Union, I do not wish to see her degraded or defaced as a member of this confederacy."

Such was Mr. Clay's policy — say rather, his humanity — whenever unanimity could be gained by concession and kindness. He was not the man to force his point in an offensive manner, or heedlessly to exasperate. And in the sober light of approaching age, his opinions of war were modified from the bold stand which he took in the ardor of his youthful patriotism. The details of his conciliatory plan were nurtured by consultation with practical men, as well as politicians; and its passage was secured by personal interviews and private conversation, as much as by public efforts.

Here was still another subject upon which Mr. Clay proved himself entitled to the name of " The great Pacificator." The government of France, in 1831, agreed, by treaty, to pay the United States Government twenty-five millions of francs for aggressions upon American commerce, subsequent to 1800. The first instalment, by the terms of the treaty, was to be paid in 1832. The draft of the United States was dishonored by the French Minister of France, no provision having been made to meet it. The President recommended to Congress to pass an act authorizing reprisals upon French property, in case provision should not be made by the French Chambers at their next session, for the fulfilment of the treaty. The subject was referred to the Committee of the Senate on Foreign Relations, of which Mr. Clay was Chairman. Great anxiety had existed throughout the country at a posture of affairs so threatening; but Mr. Clay's report, of which the Senate ordered the printing of twenty thousand copies, restored public confidence. It concluded with a resolution that it was inexpedient to vest authority in the Executive to make reprisals. This resolution was amended to read as follows: "That it is inexpedient, at present, to adopt any legislative action in regard to the state of affairs between the United States and

France." The resolution as amended, the amendments being cordially accepted by Mr. Clay, was passed unanimously. The country was saved from war, and the difficulty between France and the United States was subsequently arranged through the mediation of England.

CHAPTER XX.

PRESIDENTIAL ELECTIONS—MR. CLAY'S DEMEANOR UNDER
DISAPPOINTMENT — RESIGNATION OF HIS SEAT IN THE
SENATE.

MARTIN VAN BUREN, of New York, succeeded
General Jackson in 1836, as President of the
United States. Mr. Clay was desired to accept the
nomination in competition with Mr. Van Buren,
but declined. Mr. Van Buren received 170 out
of 294 electoral votes, General Harrison receiving
73, the next highest number. The other votes
were divided among White, Webster, and Man-
gum. At the next election, in 1840, Mr. Clay
was not a candidate, the choice of the Whig National Convention falling on General Harrison.
Harrison was elected by 234 votes, Mr. Van
Buren receiving 60. It was a matter of deep
regret with a great portion of the American people, that Mr. Clay did not receive the nomination;
and, between the announcement of the name of

the candidate and the time of the election, there was quite a disposition to put Mr. Clay up, notwithstanding the action of the Convention which nominated Harrison. But Mr. Clay exerted his influence promptly to check any such demonstration. His personal wishes were secondary to his attachment to the principles of which he considered himself the representative; and he cheerfully consented that those principles should triumph under the name of the candidate who, it was supposed, would promise more certainty of victory. We cannot resist the impression now, so triumphant was Harrison's election, that Clay would have been chosen, had he been nominated. Experience has, however, demonstrated that the most able and active men in the civil service of the country, by the conscientious performance of duty, make opponents of fractions of the people, while the nation as a whole may applaud; and the malcontents unite to defeat the election of the man of note and power.

General Harrison died in a month from the day of his inauguration, and Mr. Tyler, the Vice President, filled his term of office. At the next election, in 1844, Mr. Clay was put in nomination under greater disadvantages than any other candidate ever encountered. He had the political odium of two defeats to contend against; though the first, in 1824, should hardly have been counted; and in the second he had to contend against the unparalleled popularity of President Jackson. A worse discouragement than either, was the doubt which his friends threw over his prospects, by their abandonment of him in 1840. Every effort was made to secure his success in 1844, but all could not avail against the discouraging circumstances which we have mentioned, added to the fact that he had been so long talked about, though only once regularly nominated before. An undue confidence was, at a late day, given to his friends by the unexpected nomination of a candidate comparatively unknown, James K. Polk, of Tennessee. The canvassing for Mr. Clay was, notwithstanding, conducted with so much apparent enthusiasm, that his defeat was heard with mingled surprise and grief by those, who, had they suspected the need of exertion, might have given a different result to the contest.

Mr. Clay bore his misfortune—for a misfortune it was — with great equanimity. It is not to be supposed that he did not deeply feel the defeat.

But there were many circumstances of relief in the result. Though Mr. Polk received 170 electoral votes, and Mr. Clay only 107, yet the popular vote for Mr. Clay was larger by many thousands, than General Harrison received in 1840. And the expressions of attachment and of regret which were conveyed to him, official and individual, and the evidences of esteem which he received from all sections of the Union, showed the singular anomaly of one personally better beloved than any other public man living, yet still unable to carry the popular vote against party tactics.

In the canvass of 1848, many of Mr. Clay's friends still adhered to their old friend and first choice. Meanwhile, a new candidate for the highest office in the gift of the people, had been thrust upon public attention. Without seeking, without as much as dreaming of the possibility of a nomination to the Presidency, General Zachary Taylor was spontaneously nominated in various sections of the country, as the popular candidate for the Presidency. His brilliant military successes, his amiable heartiness and simplicity of character, his marked position as a hero and popular idol, gave him a prestige of success, which the Whig National Convention at Philadel-

phia did not feel at liberty to slight.   After four
ballotings, General Taylor received the nomination.   He was elected by 163 votes over General
Cass, who received 127.   Mr. Clay must have
been more than human, not to have felt this
neglect; but, as on previous occasions, he dis-
played his true magnanimity; for if he did not
obtrude himself as the advocate of the nomination, he positively interdicted the putting forward
of his name as a candidate — a step which some
of his friends were on the eve of taking.   Mr.
Clay never advocated the preference of military
over civil claims for civil office.   The honest opposition which he made to General Jackson, and
his course in the election, which resulted in the
choice of Adams, show that he might not have
favored Taylor as President, even though he had
no personal interest in the matter.

Having now connectedly reviewed the later
Presidential elections, in which Mr. Clay was
interested, we resume the sketch of his Senatorial labors, and more immediate personal history.
During the twelve years preceding his death, Mr.
Clay labored as earnestly for the good of his
country, as if he had not been a comparatively
unrewarded public servant.   We have preferred

to dwell at most length upon his early life, since it is chiefly for his young countrymen that we are writing; and to such, it is presumed that the account of his beginnings in life will be alike most interesting and useful.

The death of General Harrison obstructed the measures and the policy contemplated by the leading statesmen in the party who had elected him. The succession of Mr. Tyler exhibited opinions held by that gentleman, for which Mr. Clay and his friends were entirely unprepared. Mr. Clay remained in the Senate until the close of March, 1842, actively and earnestly employed in the furtherance of the measures which he deemed the exigencies of the country required, and then, in pursuance of a resolution which the death of General Harrison had deferred, resigned his seat, retiring, as he supposed, from the Senate for ever. His farewell address was most impressive and manly. He frankly acknowledged the ardor and warmth of temperament, which might have made him, in some cases, exceed the limits of courtesy; and while he tendered apologies to all whom he might have offended, declared, without exception and reserve, that he retired from

18*

the Senate without carrying with him a feeling
of resentment and dissatisfaction.

At the close of the address, Mr. Preston moved
an adjournment. He remarked that what had
just taken place, was an epoch in their legislative
history; and from the feeling which was evinced,
he saw that there was little disposition to attend
to business. The adjournment was carried, but
still the members kept their seats. Mr. Clay rose
and moved towards the area, and slowly and
reluctantly the Senate dispersed, as if loth to
believe that the voice to which they had so often
listened, was no longer to be the life of their
debates.

An affecting and pleasant incident marked the
occasion. For several years there had been an
estrangement between Clay and Calhoun. The
two old and early friends met. Their eyes filled,
recent differences were forgotten, and, with a cordial grasp of the hand, and with a mutual inter-
change of good wishes, they departed.

CHAPTER XXI.

MR. CLAY'S WITHDRAWAL FROM PUBLIC LIFE — ANNEXA-
TION OF TEXAS — THE TARIFF — LIBERALITY OF MR.
CLAY'S FRIENDS — SPEECH ON THE IRISH FAMINE —
DEATH OF HENRY CLAY, JR. — MR. CLAY'S BAPTISM —
HIS JOURNEYS — SPEECH ON COLONIZATION.

FOR seven years from the time of his resignation, Mr. Clay lived in private life. One year
of his Senatorial term remained when he retired
to Kentucky. But of the life of such a man as
Mr. Clay, no part could be strictly said to be in
retirement; for wherever he moved, the enthusiasm of the people and the warmth of friendship followed him. In the recess which he took
from public labor, he made a journey through
several of the Southern States, arriving at Washington in the spring of 1844 — the first time, we
believe, that he ever visited that city as a private
citizen. His journey was one series of public
receptions; and his opinions on topics of public
and national interest were very much sought,
and as freely given.

Mr. Clay returned in May, 1844, to Ashland, and in connexion with his arrival in Kentucky, a pleasant and characteristic anecdote is related. He had just been nominated to the Presidency, and a crowd met him at Lexington, resolved to hear their favorite speak, and to give him a Kentucky welcome. It was on Saturday evening, and he told the multitude he was happy to see them — happy to see every one of them — but there was an excellent old lady in the neighborhood whom he had rather see than any one else! So, bidding them good night, he pressed on for his home.

Mr. Clay never was reserved in the expression of his opinions. He was too frank to have any concealments, and thus presented many assailable points to opponents who perverted his words. The annexation of Texas began at this time to be mooted, and Mr. Clay, in letters, in speeches, and in conversation, declared against it, predicting, as a necessary consequence, the war with Mexico which followed that measure. The annexation was consummated under President Tyler. The election came on, and Mr. Polk, as Mr. Tyler's successor, inherited the war which Mr. Clay had predicted. The tariff, which had been temporarily adjusted during Mr. Tyler's administration, was revised under Mr. Polk, and the present system established, of which it is sufficient for us to say that it is a departure from the system which Mr. Clay had so long defended. These and other measures which are at war with the policy of Mr. Clay, were carried during his absence from the Senate. His presence in that body would not, perhaps, have averted the departure from his line of policy. A strong majority was against him; but still it is a significant fact, that the "black tariff" of 1828 and the tariff of 1846, the two most objectionable enactments on the subject, were both passed in his absence.

In rural and legal pursuits, and the restoration of his pecuniary affairs, which attention to the public weal, and too great confidence in others had impaired, Mr. Clay passed the season of his absence from public life. One of the most grateful events of his life, was the unsought contributions on the part of his friends, to relieve his estate from claims to which it had become liable by endorsing for another. The amount was over twenty thousand dollars. Well might he exclaim, in view of the bitterness with which his opponents pursued him, and the liberality and affection of his friends, " Had ever man such enemies — had ever man such friends, as I have !"

Our limits do not permit us to notice a tithe of the testimonials of respect and affection which Mr. Clay received from all classes. Some of these were of great value; as for instance, the medal presented by his friends in New York, the workmanship of which alone cost over two thousand dollars. Others were significant from their particular occasion, as the testimony of the gratitude of the sons of Ireland, for his eloquent speech in behalf of their famine-stricken countrymen. Being in New Orleans early in 1847, he was invited to attend a meeting held in behalf of Ireland; and his speech was worthy of the theme and of the man. The effect of the speech was electric on those who heard it, and on the public ear it fell great among the many great appeals which that occasion called forth. The honored of the South American patriots became beloved among the sufferers in Ireland. In the letter begging his acceptance of their testimonial — a service of splendid cutlery — the donors said, " It must be an abiding joy to your generous heart, to know that American benevolence is devoutly blessed in parishes and cabins, where even your name, illustrious as it is, had hardly been heard before the famine; and that thousands have been impelled, by their deliverance from the worst effects of that dire calamity, to invoke blessings on the head of Henry Clay."

While ever ready to commiserate the woes of others, Mr. Clay has had, in his own household, many sorrows. Of eleven children, four only survive him; and one of these, his eldest son, has been for many years the inmate of a retreat for the insane. One of his sons, Henry Clay, jr., fell at Buena Vista, while gallantly leading his men. He was a graduate of West Point, and the highest testimony is borne to his character as a soldier and a man. His loss was Mr. Clay's direct share in the miseries of the war which he deprecated; and on no occasion could he afterward allude to it, without the deepest emotion.

Following the reception of the news of this great affliction, we find Mr. Clay making a public profession in baptism of his faith in the Christian religion. His father, as we have noted, was a clergyman — his brother is also; and they both are members of a denomination — the Baptist — which does not recognize the validity of the sacrament administered to infants. From this circumstance arose the fact that the veteran statesman, in his seventieth year, was, with his daughter-in-law and four of his grand-children, admitted by baptism into the church. It was a touching testimony to the consolations, which truly great minds find in the profession of Christ, that Mr. Clay, the idol of a great nation, should bow, in his age, like a little child, and with little children, before Him who is no respecter of persons. His life needed only this to give him the highest claim to the love and veneration of his compatriots. The sacrament was administered by the Rev. Edward F. Berkely, of Christ (Protestant Episcopal) Church, Lexington, where for many years Mr. Clay had been a worshipper.

In the winter of 1847–8, Mr. Clay was drawn to Washington on professional business. The amount of physical and mental labor of which he was at this time capable, is wonderful, when we consider his advanced age. He had, during the season previous, visited New Orleans and returned to Ashland, and thence gone to Cape May, and returned, again to leave for Washington. His journeys, it must be remembered, were not the quiet passages of an unknown man; but at every considerable point he had speeches to make—often without previous notice.

Oratory was his element, and on fitting occasions he could not resist, though when necessity exacted, he could dismiss thousands in good humor with a word. In Baltimore, on one occasion, when the house in which he was a guest was besieged by his admirers, he offered them, in playful terms, a "*compromise.*" If they would let him alone, he would let them alone. He dismissed a throng in Philadelphia with similar badinage. Wit and humor were as ready with him as pathos. An amusing instance occurred during Jackson's administration. Mr. Van Buren as Vice-President, presided in the Senate. Mr. Clay, in the most pathetic terms, depicted the distress of the country, and begged Mr. Van Buren, since he had the President's ear, to make the representation to General Jackson. On the next morning Mr. Clay gravely asked him, "Well, Mr. Van Buren, did you carry my message?" At Mrs. Polk's table, in Washington, Mr. Clay said, "No one complains of your administration, madam — but I have heard *some* complaint of your husband's."

While in Washington, in 1848, Mr. Clay made one of his most splendid speeches in behalf of the

Colonization Society, at its anniversary meeting. It was remarkable no less for its retrospective facts, than for its eloquence. We may note here that in 1849, when the subject of emancipation and colonization was before the people of Kentucky, in connexion with a revision of their Constitution, Mr. Clay addressed a letter to them, advocating the same policy which he had defended, on a similar occasion, nearly fifty years before. He wished the principle of gradual emancipation incorporated in the new instrument. His appeal was unsuccessful. This circumstance affords another proof of the practical and broad philanthropy of the man. He never defended slavery in the abstract,—and was therefore denounced, by ultra pro-slavery men, as an abolitionist. He knew the South, and understood what appeared feasible, and what not, and declined to destroy his general usefulness, by limited pursuit of one idea. This caused the ultra opponents of slavery to denounce him on the other hand. His broad and statesmanlike views embraced the whole subject, in all its bearings and difficulties; and by this course, while the over-zealous condemned him, the judicious admit, that with a majority of statesmen like Mr. Clay, the evil of slavery would be gradually, as thus only it can be safely, abated.

CHAPTER XXII.

MR. CLAY RETURNS TO THE SENATE — THE COMPROMISE
OF 1850 - - THE RIVER AND HARBOR BILL OF 1851.

MR. CLAY was unanimously chosen a Senator
of the United States for the term commencing on
the 4th of March, 1849. He had previously been
offered the appointment to fill a vacancy, but declined, though he did not feel at liberty to slight
the unanimous wish of his constituents, as expressed by their choice without a dissenting voice.
The peculiar position of public affairs, and the
indications of a new collision between the North
and South upon the slavery question, no doubt
influenced Mr. Clay's course; and the service he
rendered in Congress gave him, at the close of
his life, a new title to the national gratitude.

Texas had been annexed in his absence from
Congress; the Mexican war had closed with a
new and immense accession of territory, including the disputed boundaries of Texas, which

had led to the war between Mexico and the United States. And now came the same boundary dispute between the United States and Texas, the lands in question having been ceded to the United States by the Treaty with Mexico. The last session of Congress under Mr. Polk's administration, was spent in a struggle relative to the organization of Territorial governments in the newly acquired country. The House of Representatives, in 1848, passed a resolution, as proposed by Mr. Wilmot, of Pennsylvania, and since called by his name, declaring that no territory, acquired from Mexico at the close of the war, should be open to the introduction of slavery. This "proviso" was rejected by the Senate. The session of 1848–9 went by without the settlement of the territorial government question, the House insisting upon the interdiction of slavery, and the Senate rejecting any such restriction.

On the 29th of January, 1850, Mr. Clay introduced into the Senate of the United States a series of resolutions, for the settlement of the questions in controversy. The first provided for the admission of California into the Union. The second declared that as slavery did not exist by law, and was not likely to be introduced into any of the territory acquired from Mexico by treaty, legislation on the subject was unnecessary. The third and fourth resolutions fixed the boundary of Texas, and provided for the payment to Texas of a sum afterward to be fixed for the relinquishment of New Mexico. The fifth resolution declared the *inexpediency* of abolishing slavery in the District of Columbia, while it still existed in Maryland. The sixth resolution declared the expediency of prohibiting the slave trade in the District. The seventh declared the necessity of providing, by law, for the delivery of fugitive slaves; and the eighth denied the jurisdiction of the United States over the slave trade between slave States.

After several days' debate, Mr. Clay having supported his propositions by a two days' speech, the whole subject was referred to a committee of thirteen, of which Mr. Clay was Chairman. The committee reported on the 8th of May, and their report was debated for nearly three months. The leading Senators all spoke upon it. The bill accompanying the report was called, in familiar language, " The Omnibus Bill," from the great variety of subjects which it embraced. The admission of California, the boundary of Texas, the right of new States formed out of Texas to be admitted without regard to slavery, and the establishment of Territorial governments for Utah and New Mexico, all were included in this cumbrous bill. The only part left after three months' debate, was the section establishing a government for Utah. California was afterwards admitted by a separate act. In separate bills, the rest of the subjects were also disposed of. New Mexico was organized, the limits of Texas were defined, and acts were passed for the abolition of the slave trade in the District of Columbia, and for the arrest of fugitive slaves.

Mr. Clay labored as far as his health would permit, in the business of this very laborious session. But he was no longer the indefatigable legislator. Physical debility, arising from increasing age, impaired his powers, and lessened his capacity for endurance. During the month of August he was necessarily absent, endeavoring, by repose and medical treatment, to restore his exhausted energies.

The Compromise measures formed the last important public business in which Mr. Clay took an active part. His sentiments upon the subject of slavery, and his desire for its gradual abolition, we have already exhibited. He stood before Congress in the Compromise debate, as a slaveholder, and the representative of slaveholders ; and from his speeches, we know that the concessions made by the South in the matter, though less than Mr. Clay desired, were more than any other states-man could have procured. Mr. Clay believed in the right of Congress to abolish slavery in the District of Columbia, as he showed, by simply denying its *expediency* — leaving the matter of right out of the question. But his Southern compatriots avoided any expression, by resolu-tion, which could convey this sentiment, even by implication. So far as slavery is touched in the " Compromise," no new right is claimed for the South ; the restoration of fugitives being guaran-tied by the Constitution. The surrender of the slave trade in the District, is a concession which impliedly abandons the defence of the traffic — a concession, the importance of which, in a moral point of view, is much better understood and felt at the South, than the North ; and to the South, the North owes a much higher appreciation of this concession, than it has received. And as to slavery in the new territory, California has shown what is likely to be the result of leaving its legality, or illegality, unaffirmed. Mr. Webster and Mr. Clay, with other eminent men, coincided in the opinion, that this point of slavery will adjust itself. Mr. Clay said, in introducing the subject: " From all that I have heard or read, from the testimony of all the witnesses I have seen or con- versed with, from all that has transpired or is transpiring, I do believe, that not within one foot of the territory acquired by us from Mexico, will slavery ever be planted; and I believe it could not be done, even by the force and power of public authority." Such were Mr. Clay's opinions. Such also were Mr. Webster's, who expressed them in terms even more emphatic.

Mr. Clay returned to Kentucky during the recess of Congress. He came again to Washing- ton to attend the next session of Congress, but did not appear in his seat until the 16th of De- cember. He took little part in the proceedings of the Senate, being drawn to Washington more, probably, to watch the operation of the Compro- mise policy, than from any other motive. Upon the occasion of presenting some petitions for a revision of the Tariff, Mr. Clay made some de- cided, but temperate remarks. But, on the pas- sage of the River and Harbor Appropriation Bill, the fire of old seemed to be reawakened. It was not taken up until the first day of March, three days only before the close of the session; and its opponents defeated it by questions of amendment and other party manœuvres, consuming the time till the session was closed. Mr. Clay spoke earnestly, but in vain, and the bill was laid over, unacted upon.

Among the first efforts of Mr. Clay in Congress, as the reader will doubtless recollect, were speeches in advocacy of "Internal Improvement." He first procured the formal declaration of the principle, by a resolution offered by him in February, 1807, and passed almost unanimously. And in March, 1851, his voice was heard for the last time in the Capitol, defending the policy of which he had commenced the advocacy forty-five years before.

How had the times changed since then! Many of his early co-laborers had long been in their graves; and of those who continued a long political life with him, the last survivors were dropping away. J. Q. Adams, who shared with him labor and undeserved obloquy, had but lately descended to the tomb. Calhoun, his early friend, died during the discussion of the Compromise bill. Calhoun, Clay and Webster, all participated in the labors of that famous session. All were members of the Senate in 1850 — all are now in the grave.

CHAPTER XXIII.

MR. CLAY'S LAST ILLNESS — INTERVIEW WITH KOSSUTH —
HIS DEMEANOR IN THE SICK-ROOM — HIS DEATH.

WE are now drawing to "the last scene of all."
Mr. Clay returned to Washington with the intention to resume his seat in the Senate, at the commencement of the session of 1851–2. But the
condition of his health was such, that he was
unable to take any part in the public business.
The recess had been calmly passed at Ashland;
and if Mr. Clay had been governed by motives
of selfish prudence, he would not have ventured
upon the journey to Washington.

While he was confined to his sick chamber,
Louis Kossuth, the Hungarian orator, visited
Washington, by invitation of Congress. His
speeches, wherever he had travelled in the United States, had awakened an enthusiasm in his
behalf, almost unprecedented; and not a few of
the members of the national legislature partook

of the feeling. During a previous session, Mr. Clay had opposed a resolution offered by Senator Cass, for suspending diplomatic intercourse with Austria, and had indicated, as a much better mode of showing sympathy for Hungary, the extension of relief to the exiles driven out by Austrian oppression. He exposed the danger and impolicy of becoming entangled in European politics, and defended the settled policy of the United States "non-intervention in the affairs of other nations." And when Kossuth arrived in Washington, Mr. Clay gracefully and eloquently expressed the same opinions, at an interview to which the illustrious Hungarian was admitted in his apartment. This was the last act of Mr. Clay's life which had any bearing upon public measures, if we except his acquiescence in the nomination of a Presidential candidate, made by the Whig party. His own choice had been different; but, as on previous occasions, he was ever ready to waive his personal preferences, where no sacrifice of principle was involved in the surrender.

Mr. Clay died on the morning of the 29th of June, 1852, in the seventy-fifth year of his age. His death was occasioned by a decay of his physical powers, precipitated by his intense labors during the passage of the third great Compromise.

The following account of Mr. Clay's demeanor in the sick room, is by Rev. C. M. Butler, of Washington : ·

"At the time when he was very feeble, and not expecting to survive but a few days, (though he afterwards rallied,) I was in the habit of visiting him every day. This visit was made in the afternoon. At that time, although he was able to be off his couch but about two hours, he was in the habit of being dressed as carefully, even to his boots and his watch, as if he were about to go to the Senate Chamber — a habit which showed his love of neatness and order, and which it required a vast amount of energy to sustain — and then to see his friends before and after dinner. It so happened that on one occasion when I called, I found him so exhausted that he was in haste to return to his bed, and was unable to join with me in my usual religious service. For several days after I was prevented from seeing him by parish duty. Mr. Clay sent for me, and expressed the fear that I had not been to see him, because he might have seemed irritable and impatient when I was last with him. I assured him that I had not observed the slightest evidence of anything but excessive weariness, and had been detained by unavoidable duty elsewhere. In the kindest terms he enjoined me not to allow him to become troublesome. So considerate — so kind — so humble — so fearful of wounding and giving trouble — how could it be otherwise, than that the favored group who were permitted to minister at his bed-side, learned to love him with singular tenderness and tenacity of affection ?"

Rev. Dr. Butler was a frequent visiter at Mr. Clay's bed-side, and, at his request, held religious services in his apartment, at one time, as often as once a day. The account of his last reception of the Lord's Supper, has a mournful, yet delightful interest. " Being extremely feeble, and desirous of having his mind undiverted, no persons were present but his son and servant. It was a scene long to be remembered. There, in that still chamber, at a weekday noon, — the tides of life all flowing strong around us, — three disciples of the Savior, — the minister of God, the dying statesman, and his servant, a partaker of the like precious faith, commemorated their Savior's dying love. He joined in the blessed sacrament with great feeling and solemnity, now pressing his

20

hands together, and now spreading them forth, as words of the service expressed the feelings, desires, supplications and thanksgivings of his heart. After this, he rallied, and again I was often permitted to join with him in religious services, conversation, and prayer. He grew in grace, and in the knowledge of our Lord and Savior Jesus Christ. Among the books that he read most, were Jay's Morning and Evening Exercises, the Life of Dr. Chalmers, and the Christian Philosopher Triumphant in Death. His hope continued to the end, though true and real, to be tremulous with humility, rather than rapturous with assurance. When he felt most the weariness of his protracted sufferings, it sufficed to suggest to him that his Heavenly Father doubtless knew that, after a life so long, stirring, and tempted, such a discipline of chastening and suffering was needful to make him meet for the inheritance of the saints; and at once the words of meek and patient acquiescence escaped his lips. Exhausted nature at length gave way.

"On the last occasion when I was permitted to offer a brief prayer at his bedside, his last words to me were, that he had hope only in Christ, and that the prayer which I had offered for His pardoning love, and his sanctifying grace, included everything which the dying need.   On the evening previous to his departure, sitting an hour in silence by his side, I could not but realize, when I heard him in the slight wanderings of his mind to other days and other scenes, murmuring the words, 'My mother, mother, mother;' and saying, 'My dear wife,' as if she were present.   I could not but realize then, and rejoice to think how near was the blessed reunion of his weary heart with the loved dead, and with her.   Our dear Lord, gently smooth her passage to the tomb. who must soon follow him to his rest, whose spirits even then seemed to visit and to cheer his memory and his hope.   Gently he breathed his soul away into the spirit world.

> 'How blest the righteous when they die!
>   When holy souls retire to rest,
>   How mildly beams the closing eye
>   How gently heaves the expiring breast!
>   So fades a summer cloud away,
>   So sinks the gale when storms are o'er·
>   So gently shuts the eye of day,
>   So dies the wave upon the shore.' "

CHAPTER XXIV.

SPEECHES IN CONGRESS — FUNERAL HONORS — BURIAL AT
LEXINGTON — CONCLUSION.

THE intelligence of the decease of Henry Clay
was instantly circulated, and both Houses of Congress adjourned before any formal report was communicated to them.   IIis death — long as it
had been expected—was not so immediately anticipated.   On their way to the Capitol, the members heard the rumor, and met only to adjourn.

On the next day, in the Senate, Mr. Underwood, Mr. Clay's colleague, formally announced
his death, and proceeded in a graceful eulogy.
Other Senators followed : Messrs. Lewis Cass,
R. M. T. Hunter, John P. IIale, Jeremiah Clemens, James Cooper, William II. Seward, G. W.
Jones, and Walter Brooke.   Men of all parties
and shades of political opinion, and representing
various sections of the country, and different
interests, were unanimous in their award of high
honor to Henry Clay.   In the IIouse of Repre-

THE TORCH-LIGHT POCESSION.

sentatives, Mr. Breckenridge announced the decease of the illustrious Senator. From his speech we extract one paragraph, which places Mr. Clay in a truly noble light. His countrymen, of all parties, will endorse it : —

" The life of Henry Clay is a striking example of the abiding fame which surely awaits the direct and candid statesman. The entire absence of equivocation or disguise in all his acts, was the master-key to the popular heart; for while the people will forgive the errors of a bold and open nature, he sins past forgiveness who deliberately deceives them. Hence Mr. Clay, though often defeated in his measures of policy, always secured the respect of his opponents, without losing the confidence of his friends. He never paltered in a double sense. The country never was in doubt as to his opinions and his purposes. In all the contests of his time, his position in great public questions was as clear as the sun in a cloudless sky. Standing by the grave of this great man, and considering these things, how contemptible appears the mere legerdemain of politics! What a reproach is his life on that false policy, which would trifle with a great and upright people. If I were to write his epitaph, I would inscribe, as the highest eulogy, on the stone which shall mark his resting place, 'Here lies a man who was in the public service fifty years, and never attempted to deceive his countrymen.'"

Twelve of the members of the House followed Mr. Breckenridge—representing, as in the speeches of the Senators, every class of the American people. If we were to select honorable specimens of Congressional oratory, we could find no fitter speeches than those — honorable as they are to the patriotism, the feeling, and the justice of Mr. Clay's opponents, as well as his political friends. The nation endorses the verdict on the Noble Man whose declaration was, "I would rather be RIGHT than PRESIDENT."

On Thursday, July 1, the remains of Henry Clay were removed from the National Hotel to the Senate Chamber, attended by a long funeral cortege, civil and military. The Rev. Dr. Butler read the Burial Service of the Episcopal Church, which includes the greater part of the XVth Chapter of the 1st Epistle to the Corinthians. He pronounced also a solemn and impressive discourse, founded on the seventeenth verse of the forty-eighth chapter of Jeremiah: "How is the strong staff broken and the beautiful rod!" We have already quoted from the discourse in a previous chapter, and here subjoin the closing words — the religious life of the illustrious deceased having just been reviewed by the reverend orator : —

" Be it ours to follow him in the same humble and submissive faith to heaven. Could he speak to us the counsels of his latest human and of his present heavenly experiences, sure I am that he would not only admonish us to cling to the Savior, in sickness and in death, but abjure us not to delay — to act upon our first convictions, that we might give our best power and full influence for God, and go to the grave with a hope unshadowed by the long worldliness of the past, and darkened by no films of fear and doubt resting over the future. The 'strong staff is broken,' and the ' beautiful rod' despoiled of its grace and bloom, but in the light of the eternal promise, and by the power of Christ's resurrection, we joyfully anticipate the prospect of seeing that broken staff erect, and that beautiful rod clothed with celestial grace, and blossoming with undying life and blessedness in the paradise of God."

Soon after the close of the service, the remains of Mr. Clay, suitably attended by Senators deputed for that office of mournful honor, left Washington for Baltimore. Here for the night the body lay in state, in the rotundo of the Exchange, a military corps, the Independent Grays, being its guard of honor. Thousands passed through the building to look their last upon the remains of the patriot; and a feeling of the deepest sorrow seemed to pervade the city.

On Friday evening the funeral cortêge reached Philadelphia. It was met, at the railroad depôt, by the marshals and other officers appointed by the municipal authorities of Philadelphia and the districts. The body was removed to a hearse appropriately decorated, and drawn by six dark horses, all the appointments intended, so far as funeral magnificence can go, to testify the deep grief of Philadelphians for his death, and their respect for his memory. A procession two miles in length followed the hearse. The Philadelphia Washington Grays preceded the body as an escort, and the First City Troop followed as a guard of honor. The line was formed of municipal bodies, delegations from other cities and States, societies of various names, the clergy in carriages, citizens mounted and on foot. Conspicuous, and most imposing by their numbers and appearance, were the Firemen of the city and county, who appeared in citizen's dress, wearing uniform suits of black, with white vests and gloves, and bearing torches and appropriate transparencies and banners, which much enhanced the solemn effect. Bands of music played dirge-like airs, the bells tolled, minute-guns were fired; and, save these sounds and the heavy fall of so many thousand feet, nothing broke the silence of the night. No voice was heard — no accident of any nature marred the deep solemnity of the scene.

It was midnight when the head of the procession reached Independence Square. The coffin was borne by the pall-bearers, preceded by the Chief Marshal, and the Clergy in robes, and followed by the Congressional and other Committees, up the main avenue to the Hall of Independence, where the corpse was laid in state, upon a bier, adorned with natural flowers. And here in the Hall, where a few years before Mr. Clay so touchingly alluded to the death of Mr. Adams, and where the remains of that distinguished patriot rested, Mr. Clay's body lay in state. The body was surrendered in a feeling speech, by the Chief Marshal, Major Fritz, into the keeping of the City Authorities. The Chairman of the Committee of Arrangements, Mr. Wetherill, was so overcome by his feelings, that he could not reply. As each one of the spectators admitted, passed around the bier, and took a last look at the coffin, then encircled in a wreath of green, and rare flowers, the silence of death pervaded the room. Tears were freely shed, and the deepest sorrow was depicted in every countenance.

Again at New York the funeral train made a pause, and on Monday moved again for Albany. During the stay in New York, over thirty thousand persons passed through the City Hall, looking, as they moved, upon the sealed coffin which contained all that remains on earth of the man so deeply loved. Thence by Albany, Rochester, Buffalo, Cleveland, Cincinnati, Louisville, to Lexington the sad procession moved — ever calling out from the heart of the people, the evidences of love and respect. Once, through the long line of his conquests, moved the remains of the conqueror of the old world, whose military renown rested on the ruins of a world laid waste. But the conqueror of the new, the subduer of hearts, won a greater victory in his death — the removal of the last trace of political bitterness, the verdict of a nation in his praise; and wherever the train approached, all else was forgotten, and all other men faded out of sight, before the memory of Henry Clay.

On Friday the tenth of July, the remains of Henry Clay were deposited in their resting place in Lexington, a concourse of at least thirty thousand people being present, and participating in the ceremonies. The funeral services were performed at Ashland, according to the rites of the Episcopal Church, by Rev. E. F. Berkely, of Lexington. A large platform draped with black cloth, was placed in front of the main entrance to the house where was placed the coffin, upon which were strewn flowers of the choicest kind: on the breast was placed the beautiful wreath made from the " Immortelle," brought from France, and presented by Mrs. Ann S. Stephens, the poetess. The civic wreath presented by the Clay Festival Association of New York, with a similar request, adorned the top, while the laurel wreath from Philadelphia, and the bouquets from Baltimore and Washington, were placed around it.

But we must cease the enumeration of the posthumous honors which he received, whose death revealed how deep was his hold upon the American heart. The last fact we have to write is the evidence which Mr. Clay left in his will, of his respect for his principle in relation to a great public question — the principle which he avowed in his youth, and re-affirmed in his age. That instrument provides that the children of his slaves, born after the 1st of January, 1850, are to be liberated and sent to Liberia — the males at the age of 28 years, and the females at the age of 25. Three years' earnings prior to their emancipation, are to be reserved for their benefit, for the purpose of fitting them out; and prior to the removal they are to be taught to read, write, and cypher. The slaves in being before 1850, are bequeathed to his family.

Henry Clay is now no longer a disputed name; he is no more the partisan, for death has made his fame the national legacy — the world's possession. The grim conqueror has wrested from *party* what was meant for *mankind*; and unborn generations who shall share the benefits which he aided to establish as unquestioned human rights, will revere his memory.

THE END.

www.ingramcontent.com/pod-product-compliance
Lightning Source LLC
Chambersburg PA
CBHW020055030726
47498CB00006B/1795